A Rapping at the Door

By Sarah A. Chrisman

Book Three in the *Tales of Chetzemoka* series

Tales of Chetzemoka series:

First Wheel in Town
Love Will Find A Wheel
A Rapping at the Door
Delivery Delayed
A Trip and a Tumble

Also by Sarah A. Chrisman:

Non-fiction:
Victorian Secrets
This Victorian Life

Anthologies:
Love's Messenger
Words for Parting
A Christmas Wish
The Wheelman's Joy
True Ladies and Proper Gentlemen
Quotations of Quality
A Bouquet of Victorian Roses

Author's Note:

In the mid-nineteenth-century, a religion known as Spiritualism emerged in America. (Oral tradition of my own family reports that my grandmother's aunt Phoebe was a Spiritualist.) The religion is still in practice and continues to have many followers. For information on Spiritualism in America today, please see the website of the National Spiritualist Association of Churches: https://www.nsac.org

At the same time Spiritualism emerged as a religion, a number of people who did not necessarily adhere to the tenants of the faith used its outward appearances for their own personal gain. These were not true followers of Spiritualism, but con artists who abused the faith of others to take advantage of people mourning for lost loved ones. For details of how historical con artists inspired elements of the story, please see the appendix at the end.

The character of Esmerelda in the following story is meant to represent one of these con artists — someone who had no true associations with the religion of Spiritualism and did not believe in its principles, but simply used it as window dressing to manipulate vulnerable people for her own personal gain.

This story is not intended in any way to criticize or cast aspersions on the true followers of Spiritualism or any other religion.

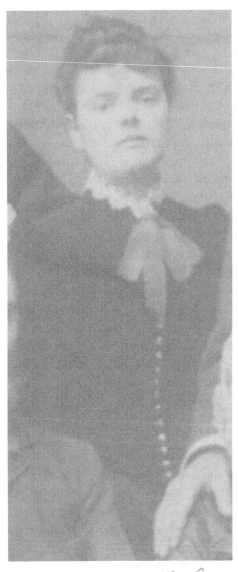

Nurse Hettie McCoy

"A detective, to be worth anything, must be at least as wily as the rogue he watches."
—Gail Hamilton, *A Battle of the Books*, 1870. p. 258.

Chapter I

October, 1882
City of Chetzemoka

Silas Hayes turned away from the bay window where he'd been watching ships leaving the harbor. He sat down in his favorite armchair by his bed and regarded the woman sitting in a smaller chair on the other side of the room, knitting. "Why is it you aren't married, McCoy?"

Nurse McCoy didn't look up from her knitting, but gave a short, dismissive laugh. "If you'd seen the men back in my part of Tennessee you wouldn't be asking that question."

"You're not in Tennessee anymore," Silas pressed her. "Washington Territory is a long way from the Smoky Mountains."

McCoy pursed her lips and glanced up at her employer, then kept knitting without comment.

Silas watched her quietly, waiting for an answer to his question.

Perceiving that he wasn't going to let the matter drop, McCoy held back an irritated sigh and plopped her knitting onto her lap. She dropped into the backwoods grammar which was only occasionally a feature in her speech now although the tones of her Appalachian accent remained as strong as they'd ever been. "Well, truth be told, I weren't never cut out to pull in double harness. Some folks just ain't, an' that's all there is to it." She fixed her bachelor employer with a disarmingly direct stare, daring him to contradict her.

Silas met her gaze for a moment, then turned away with a disappointed expression.

He looks sad, McCoy assessed. *Can't have that.*

She took up her knitting again. "Now, I don't deny that there's plenty of folks in this world who just have to marry. Take that Addie Kellam, for example, who just became Mrs. Simmons when she married your nephew yesterday. A gal with as many romantic notions in her head as she has would give herself brain fever if she didn't have an outlet for 'em. You said you liked the wedding?"

"I liked seeing the young folks so pleased with each other." He glanced out at the ships in the harbor. "I'll admit a freighter did seem like a strange place for a wedding."

Nurse McCoy smiled wryly. "Well, it was the bride's father's ship. Family traditions are often mighty strange. My cousin Ephraim got married in a cemetery."

Silas raised an eyebrow but McCoy just shrugged.

The room was quiet for a while save for the clacking of McCoy's knitting needles. Then Silas returned to the subject of the new Mrs. Simmons. "You like Adora, don't you, McCoy?"

"Of course. She's as sweet as a hogshead of Sandwich Island sugar. A body would have to have a heart of stone not to like that gal."

"She makes Jacob very happy."

"That's because he has even more romantic notions in his head than she does, although if I'd only met the gal by herself I wouldn't have thought such a thing was possible. Was he always that sentimental?"

Silas shrugged. "As far as I know. To be honest, he and I hadn't been very close before he moved here to Chetzemoka. I'm glad we've gotten a chance to get to know each other better." He paused. "Now, that you mention it, I suppose he always has had romantic notions. His mother once mentioned something to me in a letter—oh, about five years ago, I suppose it was— about how broken-hearted he was at the time over a young woman who let him court her and then ran off with a man who had more money than he did. I never pried into the details." After this story Silas frowned, placed his chin on his hand, and stared thoughtfully out the window for a long while.

After some time he turned back to McCoy. "I'm glad he met Adora, and that they'll be living here when they come back from their honeymoon."

McCoy privately agreed. She had a soft spot for the young couple, and felt they needed someone with better sense than they had to look after them. McCoy considered herself more than up to the task. Besides, it was good for Silas to have family around. Keeping track of Jacob and Addie —and their amusements with those cycles of theirs— gave him something to do besides imagining that he had every ill under the sun.

"They suit each other," Silas went on.

"They're a matched pair if I ever saw one." McCoy agreed.

There was another long pause. McCoy kept knitting.

Silas drummed lightly on the carved wooden armrest of his chair, then folded his hands in his lap. "You know, McCoy," he remarked after taking a deep breath. "It's nice when a pair start out matched, but— but plenty of horses learn to pull together alright, even if they don't seem like a set at first."

She glanced up at him. "Yeah, and a few just balk and kick all their lives if they're hitched together —to say nothing of the trouble a person can get into with ill-matched mules." She cast on a row of stitches in her knitting. "There are some beasts in this world that are born to pull in harness teams and some that the good Lord meant for saddles, and a smart man admits the difference."

She kept on with her knitting, hoping she'd managed to close the subject of why she herself had never married. She didn't like the way Silas was looking at her. It meant trouble.

When he spoke again, it was in a thoughtful, timid voice. "If you did marry, Hettie—"

McCoy scowled at her knitting.

"If you did marry, you'd have a home — forever. It means a lot to a woman to be mistress of her own home, I'm told."

McCoy pursed her lips and eyed her employer sideways. "Marrying for a home." She folded her arms and glared at Silas. "And is it a fair thing to take a man's affection —and everything he can give— and not return that affection a mite? You're suggesting I should sell myself for a roof over my head and a fire to sit by, when I've got two strong hands to earn my living? No McCoy would go in for that sort of thing."

12

"Do you think you could ever learn to —to 'return the affection', as you put it, of a man who took care of you, and was good to you?"

"It seems to me the sort of affection a woman has to learn is a poor sort. When a body has to be botherin' herself that way, it's better to let it all go." She picked up her work bag and thrust her knitting inside.

"McCoy— don't go. Please."

She tossed the bag in her lap and folded her arms again.

"I didn't mean to vex you. I'm sorry." He sighed. "You're a good woman." He regarded her a moment, then added, "You take good care of me."

She saw an opportunity to lighten the atmosphere, so she laughed. "You bet I do!" A cushion at the back of Silas' chair had gotten knocked crooked; she walked over and straightened it for him. "And I make sure you pay me well for it!"

She made a show of checking her watch. "I'd best be heading downtown if I'm going to get to the mercantile before they close. You're running shy of toilet soap."

She picked up her knitting and left the room with her customary brisk stride. She didn't look back, but she could tell that Silas watched her go.

She frowned to herself as she passed down the stairs. *I might be in for trouble while the Simmonses are gone*, she reflected, glancing back up towards Silas' room. *When men like him get lonely, they're liable to run headlong into all sorts of foolishness before they know what they're doing.*

Chapter II

On her way to the mercantile Nurse McCoy tried stopping by Dr. Brown's office to ask the doctor to pay a social call on Silas when he had the chance. Dr. Brown was the closest thing Silas had to a friend; before McCoy came he'd used to check on him several times a week. Under McCoy's care Silas' hypochondriasis had been getting so much better that the doctor had been able to cut down his professional visits to once a fortnight, but she could tell that the two men remained fond of each other on a personal level. After this morning's conversation McCoy thought it would do Silas some good to spend time with another man.

Unfortunately the doctor was out, so McCoy had to settle for leaving a note on the slate by his door and privately grumbling about the unreliability of men in general.

When she got back to Silas' house, she checked the mailbox and found a letter addressed to Mr. Jacob B. Simmons. It bore a New York postmark but had no return address.

Jacob's room was on the third floor, above his uncle's. McCoy headed upstairs intending to put the letter on his desk, but just as she reached the second floor Silas came out of his room and his eyes met McCoy's down the hallway. He startled briefly, moved to go back into his room, then paused awkwardly before turning into the hallway again.

McCoy nodded at Silas and continued up the stairs.

He looked curiously at the letter in her hand. "Mail for Jacob?" He asked, knowing that McCoy seldom went up to the third floor since her room adjoined his own on the second.

"Yep." She went back down to the second floor. "Probably more congratulations on the wedding." She peered at the address on the envelope. "Definitely a woman's writing. One of your relatives?" She passed the letter to Silas. She knew his people were from New York; Jacob and Addie were on their way there so that she could meet Jacob's parents. McCoy thought a sensible person would have saved themselves postage and waited until the couple got into town to offer their well wishes, but people could get really silly and sentimental about marriages, especially when they involved an only son.

Silas took the envelope and inspected the address. "That's not my sister's hand," he mused. "—And it's unlikely anyone from Jacob's father's family would be writing to him here. Strange."

He shrugged and began handing the letter back to McCoy, then stopped suddenly, a startled look on his face. He jerked the envelope up again and stared at the address intently. "That hand—" His voice trailed off and a sudden pallor came into his lips that McCoy didn't like.

Silas looked towards his bedroom, but frowned at the dim light coming through the east-facing windows at this time of day. He shook his head and crossed the hall into a spare room that faced west.

Very few chambers in Silas' huge mansion were actually used. Unlike some families McCoy had known where there were more people than space and a whole pack of children had to cram into one large bed, Hayes' house had far more rooms than people. Silas —a creature of very set habits— usually didn't bother with the empty rooms, and McCoy had never once seen him so much as open the door to this particular chamber in the four months she'd been in his service. She followed him, concerned.

Heavy curtains shrouded the windows in the unused room, guarding the furnishings and wallpaper from fading. Silas walked to the largest window and drew the curtains back, bathing the room in blood-red light from the setting sun. A small cloud of dust shook loose from the curtains and made him cough loudly.

Under ordinary circumstances Silas was morbidly preoccupied with his health. When he started coughing McCoy expected him to instantly retreat from the dusty room and enter into one of his customary laments about how prone his family was to consumption. When he stayed close to the window without a word about his cough, McCoy's concern deepened.

"Are you alright?"

Silas barely glanced towards McCoy. "I'm fine." He held the envelope up to the light and peered at the address. "It's very like…" He coughed distractedly.

If another man had started behaving in a fashion so contradictory to his own habits McCoy would have told him flatly that he wasn't acting "fine". However, her nursing instincts told her this was probably the least advisable comment a body could make to a hypochondriac like Silas. Instead, she asked him whose writing was on the envelope.

Silas slowly let his hand drop, then tapped the side of the envelope against his opposite palm. He sighed and shook his head, then faced McCoy. "I don't know."

"You must have some idea for it to upset you this way."

Silas frowned down at the envelope again. "It's just very strange…" He shook his head and thrust the letter at McCoy. "What I think isn't possible. Put that up in Jacob's room —we shouldn't be snooping into his mail."

McCoy took the envelope out of Silas' sight.

When she reached the third floor she didn't go into Jacob's east-facing room —not at first. Instead, she walked to a window on the other side of the house, where the light from the sunset still shone through brightly. She pressed the letter against the glass, trying to see the missive inside the envelope, but the paper was too thick for the light to shine through it. McCoy set her jaw and shook her head. *Whatever it is, it means trouble.*

McCoy didn't like trouble. Not when her patients were concerned.

She turned from the window and took the letter into Jacob's room.

Simmons' desk was a roll-top style, with a glass-fronted book case above the desk itself. McCoy tugged gently on the curved door to the writing space and wasn't surprised when it slid back easily: she'd heard Silas criticize his nephew on several occasions for the young man's habit of leaving his desk unlocked.

She placed the letter on a stack of other papers and closed the desk again, noticing as she did so that a whole shelf of the case on top of the desk was filled with books that had no titles on their spines. They were a mixture of sizes and styles, and their covers bulged out slightly from their pages, as if loose leaves had been tucked into them. McCoy guessed they were diaries. Jacob Simmons was just the sort of sentimental man who would keep a diary.

The glass front of the book case was slightly ajar. McCoy pressed it closed and left the room.

She was still wearing all her outdoor things from her trip to the mercantile. When she went back down to the second floor she stopped at her own room and took off her hat and her shoulder wrap, then switched out her chatelaine pocket for her nursing chatelaine. She felt better with her nursing chatelaine at the ready on her waist: she always felt undressed without it.

She passed through the door that connected her room with Silas' and found her employer seated in his armchair. He'd lit the lamp behind the chair and there was a newspaper in his lap, but he wasn't reading. Instead, he was staring at a small hair wreath which hung in a frame on his wall. He nervously drummed his fingers on the arm of his chair.

McCoy frowned. "Let me check your pulse," she told him. "It's good to do once in a while."

McCoy had never understood why some people grew measurably calmer when a nurse silently held their wrist for long minutes at a time. As long as she got results though, she didn't care why such silly tricks worked. All she had to know was that they did.

Silas obediently gave her his wrist. She found the pulse and stared at her brooch watch until his heart rate calmed down to a level approaching normal. Then she carefully set his hand down. "I'll bring you some lavender water. Do you want some sugar in it?"

Hayes nodded. "Please."

For a moment McCoy worried he might watch her go with that same troublesome look on his face that he had worn earlier in the day before she'd left for the mercantile. She was relieved when he didn't.

Chapter III

Dr. Brown came by after dinner and sat
talking with Silas for part of the evening. McCoy
was glad the doctor had the good sense to pretend the
visit was his own idea, and not to mention the note
she'd left him.

She left the men to themselves and retreated to
her own room to write a letter to her uncle Eb back in
Tennessee. When she heard the doctor leaving she
followed him downstairs, giving the excuse that she
needed to lock the door after him.

When they reached the front hall McCoy
handed Dr. Brown a tiny bundle of hunter green
knitting. "For your missus."

Dr. Brown looked at McCoy quizzically, then
unfolded the little package. It was a pair of baby
stockings in the same color as his cycling uniform.

Dr. Brown's eyes went wide. "Nurse McCoy!
How did you know? We weren't even truly certain
ourselves until about a week ago —we haven't told
anyone yet!"

McCoy gave a short laugh. "I was helping out
by women's bedsides soon as I was big enough to
carry hot water. I know the signs."

Dr. Brown beamed.

"Give her my compliments. Now—" She
glanced upstairs, then drew Dr. Brown into the parlor
and quietly shut the door. "How's our patient?"

Dr. Brown smiled as he put the stockings in
his jacket pocket. It took him a moment to wipe the
grin off his face, but he managed it. He finally
glanced in the direction of the stairs and grew more

serious. "You were right to ask me to come by. I haven't seen him this melancholy since before Jacob came to live here with him. I worried he might feel a little lonesome before Jacob and Addie come back next month, but I didn't expect him to get this heartsick for them so quickly. Did something happen today?"

McCoy told Dr. Brown about Silas' strange reaction to the letter that had arrived for Jacob. She didn't mention her own conversation with Silas earlier in the day.

Dr. Brown frowned thoughtfully and scratched his cheek through his whiskers. "I guess the big question is who sent the letter. It sounds like he recognized the handwriting —are you sure he didn't say or do anything that might indicate whose it was?"

McCoy shook her head. "He didn't say much of anything at all. Mostly he just looked at that hair wreath on his wall."

"I noticed him looking at it tonight, too. He told me about it once: his sister Ann —Jacob's mother— made it before she was married. The hair is hers, Silas', and both their parents'.

"He said it wasn't his sister's writing. Could it be their mother's?"

Dr. Brown shook his head. "She passed away six years ago —so did Silas' father."

McCoy sucked at the corner of her mouth. "Bad business."

Dr. Brown looked as though he might pat McCoy on the shoulder, but wisely thought better of it. "Whatever's fretting him, I'm confident you'll see him through it, Nurse McCoy. I've seen Silas go through a lot of nurses since I've been in Chetzemoka, and I have to say: you're the best of the lot. Silas knows it, too. I can tell he respects you more than any other nurse he's ever had. You know, he once threw a bowl of porridge at the last one?"

McCoy folded her arms. "I hope she threw it right back at him."

Dr. Brown smirked. "No, but I'm sure you would."

"Dumbed right I would!"

Dr. Brown chuckled. "And then you'd make him be the one to clean it up, I'm sure."

She nodded curt agreement. "Good exercise!"

He chuckled again. "Silas has been healthier these last four months than he was for years before you came, and it's not just because Jacob's been around. You're good for him."

McCoy shrugged. "Just doing my job."

"I should suggest that he raise your wages." He checked his watch. "I'd better be going. I promised Kitty I'd try to be home before she went to bed." He replaced his watch in his pocket, then patted the opposite pocket where he'd put the baby stockings. The broad grin he'd worn earlier came back to his features. "Thank you again —on Kitty's behalf."

"Don't mention it."

Chapter IV

All the rooms in Silas' impressively modern mansion had small ventilation grates near their ceilings connecting them to the adjoining rooms. Metal louvers inside the walls could be opened or shut at will to seal off unoccupied rooms or to maximize privacy of inhabited spaces. Even when they were open, these louvers blocked the view from one room to the next and prevented any light from shining through; when they were closed they blocked air and sound as well. When she'd first come to Chetzemoka, after getting over her initial astonishment at being lodged in the fancy tower room adjoining Silas' own chamber, one of the first thing McCoy had noticed about her room was that the last nurse had left the louver closed behind the ventilating grate at the top of the wall. McCoy had immediately climbed up on a chair and opened the louver behind the high, small grate between her room and Silas', and it had remained open ever since.

McCoy had always held the conviction that a nurse who sleeps more deeply than her patients isn't worth much. She knew from sounds she heard occasionally through the grate that Silas often had trouble sleeping, and like all nervous men he frequently suffered from bad dreams. Whenever she was awaked from her own light sleep by sounds of insomnia in the next room, she would dutifully sit up in bed and listen for an indication that her help was needed. Sometimes she would listen silently for hours in the dark until at last the sounds in the next room ceased and she could lay back down. She never mentioned or gave any indication that she did this, and she doubted her employer even realized she did. She herself knew she was doing a thorough job, and that was good enough for her.

Silas had never called out in the night or given signs of distress dire enough for her to enter his room on her own recognizance, but if he ever did, she'd be ready.

For several days after the conversation about marriage and the arrival of the mysterious letter, Silas remained sullen and uncommunicative. McCoy knew it was only a matter of time before he had one of his troublesome nights. She took care not to overtax herself in the day, so that she would be ready for a long vigil if necessary.

When the trouble came, it was the worst yet.

Deep in the darkest hours of night McCoy awoke to the sounds of bedsprings creaking as the occupant of the next room tossed in his sleep. She rubbed at her eyes, then very carefully sat up without making a sound. She reached over to the water glass she kept on her bedside table, lifted it silently, and took a long drink to help herself wake up.

She sat listening in the dark, occasionally taking little sips of her water when she started to feel drowsy. At first there were just the sounds of a restless sleeper, accompanied by the distant, eternal heartbeats of ticking clocks.

After a while the tossing sounds ceased. There was a swift >*swoosh!*< of bedclothes thrown back, and a sharp squeal of bedsprings as the wakened sleeper shot up into a sitting position.

McCoy sat up straighter in the dark herself, listening intently. *One of his nightmares,* she assessed. She set down her glass and waited.

For long moments there were no human sounds at all in the house, just the mechanical ticking of clocks. McCoy had to fight drowsiness again; she shook her head and blinked hard in the dark.

When McCoy started thinking she needed to hold her water glass again to keep herself awake, there was another shrill squeal of bedsprings, accompanied this time by a creaking of wood.

He stood up.

Footsteps slowly walked across the floor in Silas' room. McCoy waited patiently for a knock on her door.

The steps turned and went the opposite direction, turned again, came back, turned again.

Pacing. That's bad.

A light glimmered at the keyhole of the door that connected her room to Silas' as a small lamp was lighted. Then she heard Silas' hallway door open.

Where's he going?

McCoy pushed back her blankets, checked that her nightdress was buttoned all the way, and reached for her slippers.

The steps moved down the hallway and started climbing the stairs to the third floor.

McCoy passed into the hall and called out, "Mr. Hayes? Are you alright?"

Silence.

McCoy went to the stairs and looked up to where a faint light glimmered from the lamp in Silas' hand. "Are you alright?" She repeated.

From what she could see in the dim glow of the lamplight, his expression seemed embarrassed. He hesitated a long moment, than answered, "I'm fine. Go back to bed."

"I will after you do." She started up the stairs. "I have to practically light a fire under you to get you to move your bones in broad daylight. What are you doing climbing up to the third floor in the middle of the night?"

"Nothing!" He said it too quickly.

"Does this have anything to do with that letter that came for Mr. Simmons the other day? You said yourself you shouldn't be snooping into his mail."

"I'd thank you to mind your own business!"

She eyed him suspiciously. "You should take your own advice there."

"Fine!" He snapped angrily, and started back down the stairs.

McCoy saw him enter his room again. She returned to her own chamber, and sat down on her bed to listen.

After enough time had passed for a lazier nurse to have gone back to sleep, Silas' hallway door opened again and he started up the stairs once more.

We can't very well be repeating that scene all night long, McCoy reflected in extreme irritation. *I can stay up all night, but he'll make himself sick this way*. She glared into the dark.

Silas' quick response when she'd asked about the letter had convinced McCoy that this was exactly what he was after. She'd known that letter meant trouble.

The most common way she knew of for opening a letter on the sly was steaming it open —and unfortunately, Silas had the apparatus to do exactly that, right in his bedroom. Since the weather had turned cool enough for the stoves in their rooms to be lit in the mornings, McCoy had been bringing two kettles of water upstairs to their rooms every night before bed —one for her, one for Silas. That way they could heat water for washing over their little bedroom stoves in the morning and not have to choose between waiting for the big kitchen stove to warm up or bathing in cold water on a frigid morning.

When she heard the footsteps disappear up to the third floor, McCoy quietly opened the door that connected her room with Silas'. She found his kettle by touch in the dark and brought it back to her own room. *Bad as taking brass pins away from a baby when the little varmint tries to swallow 'em,* Nurse McCoy reflected sourly. Honestly, she didn't know how any of the fools in this world would get along without her.

Feeling comfortable that she'd done her duty in keeping Silas out of mischief for the night, McCoy went back to bed and allowed herself to fall into a deeper sleep than usual.

Chapter V

"Goll dumb it!"

McCoy frowned at the firebox of the kitchen stove, greatly irritated. She'd cleaned it out and laid a new fire the night before, same as she did every night. Yet this morning when she'd gone to light it for breakfast she'd found only ashes.

Just like a man! She reflected, annoyed. *At least a woman trying to sneak around doing something like that would have had the sense to lay a fresh fire again.* She shook her head and glared at the kettle. It was in a different position on top of the range than how she'd left it, of course. *He just had to go and steam that letter open, didn't he? That man simply can't stay out of mischief.*

The last time Silas had meddled in his nephew's affairs, McCoy had found Addie crying her eyes out in a bunch of willow bushes. McCoy'd had an irritating morning sorting things out. This business with the letter seemed like even bigger trouble.

She swept the ashes through the grate in the bottom of the stove's firebox, laid a new fire, and got it started so the stove could heat up for breakfast. Then she re-lit the fingerlamp she'd carried down from her bedroom, turned out the big kitchen lamp, and marched upstairs to give Silas a piece of her mind. He usually didn't wake up until hours after she did, but McCoy felt entitled to force an exception after he'd wreaked such havoc with her own sleep the night before.

When she reached the second floor, she heard water running. Hayes' mansion had a large tiled bathroom where each of the inhabitants indulged in a long soak in the porcelain tub several times a week. (Even McCoy was encouraged to use the fancy bathroom, to her great delight.) McCoy wasn't terribly surprised Hayes would opt for a full soak this morning: after all, she'd taken away the kettle in his room that he usually used to heat water for a bath with his ewer and basin. She was, however, quite surprised to hear him awake this early.

Did he go to bed at all, after that first time he woke me up? Concern calmed her temper and she quietly entered his bed chamber.

She thought back to when she'd woken up that morning, and tried to remember if she'd seen any light under the door that connected her room to Silas'. The thought naturally drew her gaze to the door in question, and her eye was arrested by a dark form at the bottom of the door, something that shouldn't have been there. She walked over and held her lamp so that its light fell on the unexpected shape.

It was a blanket, stuffed against the crack at the bottom of the door. After realizing what it was, McCoy peered at the keyhole and saw that the little notch had been stuffed with cotton. *Of all the silliness!* McCoy shook her head. *The man's as bad as a child. But it's no wonder I didn't notice a light.*

There were a number of lamps in Silas' room, but the one he used most was a large one with a ball shade that sat on a table between his bed and favorite chair. McCoy went over and carefully felt the lamp's chimney inside the shade. It was warm, but it didn't scorch her fingers.

Hard to tell much from that, she reflected. *Maybe it was burning for hours and it's been out long enough to cool down. Or maybe it was only burning a few minutes when he got his things together to go off to the tub —not long enough to get so very hot— but I only just missed seeing him when I came up the stairs, so it's still warm. I suppose I could heft the oil reservoir to see how full it is, but a lamp this big only gets filled a couple times a week, so four hours or so in the middle of the night won't have emptied it enough to really tell much of a difference.* She frowned, shaking her head.

She peered at the lamp's base thinking about the futility of hefting the reservoir, but then she noticed some papers on the table and the entire focus of her inquiries shifted. She held her finger lamp in a position to shine full upon the papers.

They were two letters, both open. She recognized the one addressed to Jacob Simmons by its envelope. The other was written in the same woman's handwriting, and was addressed to Mr. Silas Hayes.

McCoy paused. Holding the letter up to the window had been one thing, but this was an entirely different level of snooping, and it went against her grain. As far as she was concerned, people's lives were their own business. Not only was she not entitled to pry into other people's affairs, she truly wasn't interested in them. Most people were a mix of foolish and dull, and she had better things to do with her time than snoop into a bunch of nonsense that had nothing to do with her and would just bore her silly.

But this concerned a patient, and it was important she find out why he'd been acting so strange lately. She couldn't help him if she didn't know what was wrong.

She lifted the letter addressed to Mr. Simmons. It was very short, and she scanned its few lines quickly:

Dear Jacob,
An old friend will soon pay you a visit. Make sure you give her your full trust and confidence.
—L.H.

McCoy huffed quietly to herself. *Well, that's about as clear as oatmeal!* She reflected disdainfully.

She picked up the other letter. It was much longer, running to several pages, and was dated six years ago. McCoy's eyes went wide when she read the opening line:

My dear son,

McCoy started up in shock. She remembered what Dr. Brown had told her when she'd reported how Silas had spent the whole evening staring at the hair wreath on his wall. She looked again at the date on this longer letter, the one addressed to Silas. Then she turned to the very last page and scanned down to the signature line. It ran,

Your loving mother,

Lily Hayes.

McCoy compared the L and the H in "Lily Hayes" with the initials L.H. on the letter that had arrived for Mr. Simmons a few days ago. Then she carefully found other words the two papers had in common. The shapes of the letters were identical. The handwriting on the letter that had come for Jacob just a few days ago was unquestionably the same as the handwriting on the letter written by Silas' mother.

McCoy looked back and forth between the two letters, feeling disbelief at first, then a faint, cold chill.

L.H. —Lily Hayes, "your loving mother". And the handwriting's the same. But Dr. Brown said Silas' mother died six years ago!

Chapter VI

The house seemed quieter than it had when McCoy had come upstairs. She wondered about this briefly, then realized that the water in the bathroom had stopped running.

Silas had been breaking so many of his regular patterns McCoy couldn't guess how long he would stay in the tub soaking this morning. She did know for certain she didn't want him to find her in his room, reading private letters. *Not just his private correspondence, but Mr. Simmons' as well. Mr. Hayes would be right to think me a fine hypocrite, after I scolded him last night for snooping into other people's affairs.* She'd known nurses who'd been dismissed for less, and as far as McCoy was concerned they deserved to be.

She put the letters back on the table in positions as close as possible to the ones she remembered finding them in. Then she returned to her own room by way of the door connecting it directly to Silas' chamber. She didn't want to run the risk of him seeing her exit his room by going out into the hall.

McCoy carefully pulled the door to her room shut after herself. The bottom of the door stuck a bit on the blanket Silas had laid down in the night to block the light from his own room; McCoy hoped the blanket would fall back into a position similar enough to its former place that it wouldn't draw his suspicion.

In her own room, McCoy frowned and sucked at the corner of her mouth. Back in nursing school she'd butted heads with the ward matron on several occasions (in retrospect, McCoy realized the problem had likely stemmed from she and her being too similar for comfort), but battling personalities aside, Nurse O'Reilly had had the rare quality of good common sense. She'd drilled the idea bone deep into McCoy that when a nurse doesn't know what's wrong and the doctors can't help her, she needs to assess the facts of the case and list the things she knows for sure are true.

McCoy looked for something to do while she thought —another of Nurse O'Reilly's drills: *Patients rest: we don't.*

Her bed still wasn't made, so she started stripping the blankets. She asked herself what she knew for sure, and came up with the following list:

1. According to Dr. Brown, Silas' parents both died six years ago.

2. Silas' family was from New York.

3. A few days ago, a letter arrived for Silas' nephew, postmarked New York.

4. The handwriting on the letter seemed an exact match for the deceased Mrs. Hayes' handwriting.

5. The inexplicable strangeness of the letter was distressing Silas.

6. Silas was McCoy's charge, and she was responsible for his well-being.

McCoy snapped the last blanket onto her bed and flattened it with precision. When she straightened her back again, she felt she had determined the appropriate medicine for her patient's case. *He needs a rational explanation to set his mind at ease. I'm sure there is one.* McCoy tugged a fold in her apron straight. *I just have to find it before the man frets himself into a lunatic asylum or makes himself physically ill.*

As she went about her morning tasks, McCoy's first theory was that the "loving mother" of the older letter might not be Silas' birth mother at all, but rather an exceptionally fond step-mother. If they'd had a falling out later, it might account for his shock at seeing her handwriting again. However, when McCoy drew Silas into conversation about families in general, a few careful questions revealed that his father had pre-deceased his mother. Clearly, a step-mother was therefore impossible.

McCoy's next idea was wilder than her first, and even she admitted it was better suited to the plot of a yellow-backed novel than to real life: could Silas be mistaken about his mother's death? Could she, in fact, still be alive?

Even more careful questioning revealed that this too was impossible: Hayes had not only been present at his mother's death-bed six years ago, but he'd also seen her laid in her grave.

Hard to mistake that sort of thing, McCoy reflected. *So what else is left?* She wracked her brain, but after a while she admitted she was just plumb stumped.

A hired girl named Mary came by Silas' mansion once a week to dust, clean the floors, and generally take care of the housekeeping tasks that fell outside McCoy's duties as a trained nurse. This was cleaning day, so when Kitty Brown came to the house in the early afternoon Mary was the one who let the doctor's wife inside and announced her presence.

"At first I told her I'd let Mr. Hayes know she was here—" Mary reported to McCoy, who was mixing tamarind water in the kitchen when Mrs. Brown arrived. "—But she said it was you she'd come to see." She fidgeted awkwardly, uncertain as to whether she was doing the right thing in calling McCoy to the parlor.

Mary was only about seventeen years old, and she'd mentioned to McCoy at some point that this was her first housekeeping job. She was wonderfully capable at her cleaning tasks —even Silas admitted this, though he was usually so impossible to please. However, the lack of a real mistress in Silas' household was making it extremely difficult for the young woman to learn the finer points of her duties. Things like answering the door and announcing callers —things that really should be the more enjoyable parts of her job— made her nervous and unsure of herself. For Mary's sake McCoy was glad that (with Mr. Simmons now married) there would soon be a proper lady of the house to guide and train the young housekeeper in things that went beyond scrubbing the floors.

McCoy patted Mary's arm. She'd heard it was good to pat a person's arm when they're nervous. "It's alright, I think I know what it's about. Give me a few minutes with her, then fetch down Mr. Hayes. The company'll do him good."

As soon as McCoy appeared in the parlor, Kitty launched into rapturous thanks for the baby stockings McCoy had sent. Kitty's face was shining brighter than a camphene lamp, and she asked Nurse McCoy's opinions on all the self-same subjects that women in her condition for the first time always ask about. McCoy answered matter-of-factly, not in the least surprised Kitty was asking her these things instead of querying her husband about them. There are some things even doctors' wives prefer talking to other women about.

When Silas came down the talk shifted to his nephew's recent wedding. The Browns and the Simmonses were good friends: Dr. Brown was the president of the local cycling club and Jacob and Addie were both active members —unsurprisingly, since Jacob ran the local cycle store. The whole club had been present at the dinner after the wedding ceremony, but the ceremony itself had been a very small, family-only affair on Captain Kellam's ship and Kitty was curious to hear all the specific details about the event.

McCoy felt some slight trepidation about allowing Silas' mind to wander back to the subject of weddings, but she admitted privately that there had been a much more serious problem in the house for several days. The nervous worries Silas had contracted from the mysterious letter were posing a serious threat to his well-being. Until McCoy could determine a rational explanation and offer it up as a cure, exposure to Kitty's contagious happiness would serve as a good palliative treatment.

After they had been chatting a while, the doorbell rang. All three of them looked towards the door in surprise: Silas rarely had visitors. McCoy rose from her seat to answer the door, but Silas reminded her that Mary was there and could get it.

"It just better not be another of those dumbed patent medicine salesmen," McCoy grumbled. "I keep sendin' 'em packin', and they just keep slitherin' back like snakes."

Kitty shuddered visibly and McCoy realized the analogy had been a poorly chosen one in the present company. She'd forgotten a story Dr. Brown had told her in confidence once, about how his wife had been deathly afraid of snakes ever since one of them had spooked her first husband's horse, resulting in the man's untimely death.

Fine way to put your foot in your mouth, McCoy! Now don't just let her sit there and stew on it.

McCoy asked Kitty, "Do you think it could be the doctor at the door?"

She brightened immediately. "Maybe! Oh, no, wait—" She seemed to remember something. "He was going to check on some farmers' families out in Center Valley this afternoon. He won't be back yet."

Thinking about her current husband, Kitty smiled softly. She let her hands rest lovingly on her abdomen, where there wouldn't be any visible sign of her condition for a long time yet.

Mary came into the room then, carrying a handbill of some sort. "I wasn't sure what I should do," she told Silas. "It's not exactly a caller—" she explained, then looked towards McCoy. "—But it's not really a tradesman, either."

Kitty smiled reassuringly. "It's alright, Mary. Just give the handbill to Mr. Hayes and let him decide how to deal with it."

Mary cast her a grateful look and brought the paper over to Silas. He took it from her with the usual sour expression with which he met any slight deviation from routine, but when he read it a sudden interest filled his expression. "Who brought this?"

"The woman herself," Mary answered nervously. "—The one whose picture's on the paper there."

"And is she still here?"

"I think so."

"Send her in!"

McCoy stood up and stepped over by Silas' chair to look at the handbill. "What's going on?"

Rather than answering, he handed her the slip of paper. It ran thusly:

Mdmlle. Esmerelda Gracilis Positive, Prophetic, Healing and Trance Medium Psychrometrist, Clairvoyant, and Mineral Locator

Below this was an engraving of a woman displaying a quantity of loose hair flowing over an expanse of bare shoulder.

Kitty leaned forward curiously. "What is it, Nurse McCoy?"

"A hussy who needs to find her hairpins and put some clothes on." McCoy handed Kitty the paper then faced Silas with her hands on her hips. "If she thinks she's gonna come here amongst decent folks in my charge lookin' like that, I'll tell you right now—"

The parlor door slid open and Mary announced the woman whose name was atop the handbill.

McCoy saw her first objection was nullified right away: the woman was decently clothed and her light brown hair was neatly coiled. She was comely —even beautiful— in vaguely elfin way, and she moved with a light step that encouraged the analogy. She had large, round eyes a few shades darker than her hair, and lips like curved bows drawn by fairies. Her face was, perhaps, a trifle longer than is generally considered ideal for a woman, but nature had compensated for this slight imperfection by gifting the woman with a small, perfectly round chin and skin like milk. There was something a little too perfect about that face, and she was strongly perfumed with patchouly. McCoy stayed on her guard.

As Esmerelda entered the room McCoy noticed that she took in every detail of her surroundings, though she remained very careful to make her observations in discrete glances that went unnoticed by both Silas and Mrs. Brown. McCoy didn't wear a nurse's cap, but in the setting of Silas' fancy parlor her apron and her simple striped cotton dress marked her so clearly as a servant of some sort that Esmerelda gave her little more than a quick, cursory glance. This was fine by McCoy, since it gave her free rein to scrutinize Esmerelda's actions.

The ornate parlor with its thick oriental carpet and expensive furnishings seemed to please the woman. When she looked at the stained glass windows and the embroidered fire screen, the rosewood table with its ebony and ivory chess set, and the deeply carved wooden chairs upholstered with velvet, there was a sly, evaluating look behind her eyes that put McCoy in mind of a customer at a shop about to put in a large order.

Kitty was still seated with her hands in a telling position over her abdomen; Esmerelda noticed this and quickly had to control a small frown. When Silas introduced Kitty as Mrs. Brown, Esmerelda's carefully suppressed displeasure was replaced with a genuine smile. After she had seated herself, Silas asked what had brought her.

"My faith," Esmerelda replied with soft conviction.

"And what faith is that?" He asked.

She held a hand over her heart. "A faith in constant communication between the mortals and the occupants of the beautiful spirit-home beyond the river."

In other words, McCoy appended privately, *a faith in moving tables and spirits who can't spell properly.* Her cousin Elroy had once gone to a medium who claimed she could put him in touch with his dead wife. They used an alphabet board to communicate with her spirit, and whoever was moving that planchette around could barely spell cat. Elroy's missus had been the county spelling champion when she was a girl and had stayed proud of the fact her whole life: if her spirit really had been at the seance, she'd have thumped the phony spiritualist on the head for slandering her.

Silas leaned forwards. "Is it really possible?"

"Not only possible, but scientifically proven!" Esmerelda assured him.

McCoy started to laugh, but halfway through the action she changed it into a sneeze. Kitty frowned at her.

"Spirits…" Silas rubbed his chin thoughtfully.

Kitty swallowed nervously, then asked, "Can you really communicate with— with those who've passed on?"

Esmerelda looked at the nervous, hopeful expression on her face and smiled. "Of course."

Kitty's eyes widened, and she slowly raised a hand to her lips.

McCoy was surprised Kitty was taking this so seriously —and a little disappointed in her. She'd have expected the doctor's wife to have more sense.

"You still ain't told us what you come for," McCoy told Esmerelda pointedly.

Esmerelda placed her hand on her heart again. "The spirits sent me hither. They said there was someone here who would appreciate seeing me."

"Yeah, I'll just bet they did," McCoy muttered.

"McCoy!" Silas gave her a stern look. "Leave us."

McCoy shrugged. "Fine by me. It's gettin' late in the day to just be sittin' around, anyways."

At McCoy's mention of the time, Kitty pulled out her watch. "Oh, dear, I'm late for meeting Rachel Goldstein!" She exclaimed, standing. "I promised I'd help her fit a dress she's making for herself."

Kitty started to replace her watch in her watch in her pocket, but Esmerelda held up a hand. "Wait, my dear," she said familiarly. She pressed her fingertips to her forehead. "I believe someone wants to tell you something." She reached towards Kitty's watch. "May I?"

The watch itself was just a cheap Waterbury, but there was an intricate fob attached to it which seemed to have been taken from a man's watch chain. Kitty looked more reluctant to part with the fob than with the watch itself, yet after a slight hesitation she unfastened her watch chain from her buttonhole and handed over the whole arrangement.

While Esmerelda was making claims about spirits and Kitty was giving up her watch, McCoy noticed that Mary was still in the room. No one had thought to dismiss the housekeeper after she'd shown in Esmerelda, and the inexperienced girl had been awaiting further instructions. McCoy motioned for her to stay, then mouthed, "Dust the parlor!" She discretely pantomimed dusting motions and pointed to a far corner. Mary nodded, pulled out a dusting cloth which had been tucked into her apron strings, and quietly followed McCoy's instructions.

McCoy didn't trust this Esmerelda character alone with Silas: he was McCoy's charge, and her responsibility. If he was sending her away and Kitty was leaving, at least Mary could stay and keep an eye on him.

The exchange between the servants had gone unnoticed. Esmerelda's eyes were closed now, and she held Kitty's watch to her heart with her right hand. She pressed her left-hand, palm-upwards, against her forehead the way actresses do before they sham a faint. Silas and Kitty both watched the performance with rapt attention.

Esmerelda had pressed the watch flat to her chest, but the fob hung loose over the back of her hand. McCoy could see it was a locket with a crystal face covering two tiny, artistically curled locks of hair. One of them was blonde like Kitty's hair, but the other was the wrong color to be Dr. Brown's. McCoy guessed it was a memento of Kitty's first husband.

Esmerelda spoke in a slow, far-off voice, saying, "The one you mourn remembers you and asks— and asks that you not worry about the passage of time, for there is no time beyond the spirit river."

After this short speech Esmerelda slumped and let her hands fall into her lap. Then she opened her eyes and gazed around the room. "Oh," she said with a lost-seeming expression. "Did I say anything?"

Chapter VII

Silas eyed Esmerelda with a curious, evaluating look, as if not quite sure what to think. Kitty took back her watch with such a display of emotion that McCoy felt embarrassed for her.

McCoy took Kitty firmly by the arm, glared at Esmerelda, and marched the doctor's wife out of the room.

After the parlor door was shut and they'd retreated a few paces, McCoy turned towards Kitty. "Don't tell me you've been taken in by that humbug!" She demanded.

"But McCoy, you saw—"

"I saw a bad actress shamming some silliness. My six-year-old niece is a more convincing liar when she's caught holding an empty marmalade jar."

Kitty looked disappointed at McCoy's lack of faith. "But what she said—"

"—Was vague enough to apply to anyone. You know it was."

Kitty sighed and hung her head. After a long moment of silent frowning, she finally nodded. "I wanted to believe—" She ran her thumb over the watch fob, looking at the small wisps of hair under the crystal. Then her gaze shifted very slightly and she started. "Nurse McCoy!" She looked up, meeting McCoy's eyes. "My watch stopped!"

"Did you forget to wind it?"

"No, I'm sure I—" Mrs. Brown tried to turn the crown on the watch's stem, but it only went around a few times before halting. "See? It shouldn't have stopped until tomorrow morning. And look—"

She turned the watch face towards McCoy. "Now it's fully wound, but you can see yourself it's not working!"

The watch was the sort with a little window in its face to show off its gears, and McCoy saw that they had all frozen to a halt. "Strange..." she admitted.

Kitty glanced back towards the parlor. "What she said about there being no time in the afterlife—"

"Now, hold on!" McCoy protested. "The one ain't got nothin' to do with the other! You saw a humbug having fun and it upset you 'cuz you're in a delicate state right now. Then your cheap watch — I'm sorry, ma'am, but it *is* cheap— your cheap watch stopped working with the usual bad timing of all cheap watches. If it had happened an hour earlier you wouldn't have minded it at all."

McCoy took the watch and placed it securely back in Kitty's pocket. "Don't you fret about it! Just go help Mrs. Goldstein with her dress, buy a new watch tomorrow, and forget about the whole thing!"

Kitty frowned, then nodded uncertainly.

"Now—" McCoy squared her shoulders. "Let's get you over to Mrs. Goldstein's before you're any later than you already are!"

Kitty smiled slightly at the way McCoy was taking charge of her, but she went along complacently.

The Goldsteins were Silas' nearest neighbors; their property adjoined his. McCoy marched Mrs. Brown over there and spent a few minutes transferring charge of her to Rachel Goldstein.

McCoy liked Rachel, although she would have liked her a lot better if the woman wasn't quite so obsessed with matters of dress. Her tendency to drone on about the latest fashions could grate on McCoy's nerves but otherwise she seemed fairly sensible, and her heart was definitely in the right place. McCoy thought she might be just what Kitty needed that afternoon.

McCoy went back into Silas' house just as Mary was leaving the parlor. McCoy peeked in and saw that it was empty. "She gone?"

Mary nodded.

"Mr. Hayes upstairs?"

Mary nodded again.

"Come in the kitchen with me a minute."

When they arrived in the kitchen McCoy shut the door carefully behind them. "What were they saying in there?"

Mary frowned. "That Miss Gracilis is kind of strange…"

"Don't you bother 'Miss Gracilis'ing her. Not when you're talkin' to me. Esmerelda's good enough, although if that's her real name I'll eat my hat. What were they saying?"

"Well," Mary told her. "—There was a lot more like what you heard. Mr. Hayes kept asking if she could really talk to spirits and she kept telling him she could —it got pretty repetitive, really. He seemed worried about her because she acted like she was sick after that thing she did with Mrs. Brown's watch."

McCoy frowned. She knew Silas had a weak spot for young women he thought needed protection. Addie Kellam —the new Mrs. Simmons— had told

McCoy how the first time she met Mr. Hayes his whole attitude towards her changed after he noticed her limping. *Turned out fine that time*, McCoy remembered. *But if he's too sympathetic with this Esmerelda character it might mean trouble.*

"Go on," McCoy urged Mary.

"Well, after she got Mr. Hayes to believe her about talking to spirits, he said he wanted to talk to his mother."

McCoy remembered the strange letter, apparently written in Silas' mother's handwriting. McCoy suddenly would have given a lot to see this Esmerelda's handwriting.

Mary continued, "She asked if there weren't any other people in the house. She said something about it taking a lot of energy to contact certain spirits, and that she needed more than just herself and Mr. Hayes to do it right. Mr. Hayes said he'd get you to help—"

McCoy snorted.

"—And she said that still wasn't enough, that she needed someone else," Mary went on. "Then I spoke up for the first time and asked if I could do anything to help. Esmerelda looked down her nose at me and— well, she made a remark about half-breed servants I wouldn't care to repeat, Nurse McCoy." A strand of Mary's raven-black hair had fallen over her olive cheek. She pushed it behind her ear and frowned in irritation. "She's not from around here, saying things like that. Even you don't talk that way, and you're from *the South!*"

McCoy ignored the implied slander of her home region and urged Mary to go on with the story.

"Then Esmerelda said that for talking to spirits it was really best to have family members to help. I said that in that case she'd have to wait for Mr. and Mrs. Simmons to get back. She looked really startled when I said that. She looked over at Mr. Hayes real quick and asked what his sister's doing here.

"Then it was his turn to look surprised," Mary went on. "More than surprised, really. He looked like a galvanic shock had run right through him. He asked how she knew his sister's married name. She made a show of acting sick again then said the spirits told her."

McCoy shook her head scornfully.

Mary shrugged and went on, "They were both flustered a while, then Mr. Hayes explained it wasn't his sister and her husband I'd meant, it was their son and his new wife. Mr. Hayes said his nephew and the new Mrs. Simmons won't be back for almost another month, and he told Esmerelda he hoped they wouldn't have to wait that long to talk with the spirits. Esmerelda looked really thoughtful and said she'd have to privately ask her companion spirit for advice before doing anything. Then she left, and Mr. Hayes went up to his room. After I'd shown Esmerelda out I went back into the parlor to sweep the carpet; I'd just finished when you got back." Mary looked nervously at McCoy, waiting for approval or disapproval.

"That was a good job, Mary." McCoy assured her.

Mary smiled with relief.

"Have you pretty much finished the rest of the cleaning?"

"Nearly. I didn't go into your room or Mr. Hayes' bedroom because you said it was your job to clean those—"

"That's right."

"—And I haven't had a chance to clean the bathroom yet."

"I'll take care of that, too. You go on home. Take some of those apples off the tree outside with you, if you want some."

"Thank you."

Mary took off her apron and started to hang it on a peg by the door. As she did so she noticed a folded paper she'd forgotten in her apron pocket. "Oh, Nurse McCoy? I wasn't sure what to do with this."

She handed the paper to McCoy, who saw that it was Esmerelda's handbill.

McCoy took it and frowned. "That's alright," she told Mary. "I'll take care of this, too. You have a good week."

After Mary had gone McCoy turned towards the stove. She lifted the eye at the back of the firebox and thrust the handbill down onto the embers which still glowed there.

After replacing the stove eye McCoy shot back the bolt at the side of the firebox to feed in more air, then peered through the draft holes. She saw the spiritualist's picture engulfed by flames, then consumed by them. Finally she straightened, frowning. She had a feeling this Esmerelda character would be far more troublesome to dispose of than her handbill.

Chapter VIII

That whole afternoon and into the evening
Silas watched anxiously out his bedroom window,
waiting for Esmerelda to come back. There was
something sad about the nervous way he leaned
forwards for a better look whenever he saw someone
coming up the road, then sank back again,
disappointed, when he realized it wasn't her. He
reminded McCoy of a dog that's been abandoned at a
railway station and keeps looking for his master. She
would have felt sorry for him if the whole situation
wasn't so patently ridiculous. As things stood, she
just wished she could plant her boot in that Esmerelda
creature's backside for riling up her patient this way.

Shortly after sundown McCoy fixed Silas a
mug of warm milk with lavender and valerian added
to it, then put him to bed early. After she'd assured
herself that he was asleep, McCoy donned her warm
things and slipped quietly out of the house with a
lantern.

She wanted to discuss the case with Dr.
Brown, but she worried that if she planned on his
office hours she'd find him out on a house call again.
As she followed the steep footpath through the woods
towards the doctor's home, McCoy was confident she
would find the Browns still awake. Stars glistened in
the sky like drops of water on cold charcoal, yet for
all the darkness of the night it wasn't really very late
yet.

When she arrived at the Browns' house there
were lights visible in the parlor windows and two
bicycles leaned against the outside of the house.

Visitors from the cycling club, McCoy assessed. When she got close enough to see the figures through the window, she recognized Addie's brother Ken Kellam and his friend Felix Halloway. They were playing some sort of parlor game with the Browns.

Well, it's sure they're awake then, McCoy reflected. *This won't take but a few minutes.*

Dr. Brown saw McCoy's lantern as she approached and he met her at the door with a look of concern. "Nurse McCoy! What's—"

"No emergency," she assured him quickly. "I just wanted to talk to you and I didn't want to leave Mr. Hayes alone for an hour or more tomorrow to go downtown and then find you gone from your office."

"Alright. What's going on?"

"A queer creature came sniffin' around Mr. Hayes place this afternoon—"

Dr. Brown chuckled softly. He waved at the folks inside and told them to go on with the game, then he joined McCoy outside and shut the door behind himself. "You mean that spiritualist-magician who stopped my wife's watch this afternoon. Kitty told me about her."

"She's up to no good, I'll tell you that much!"

Dr. Brown shook his head and chuckled again. "I've been wanting to buy Kitty a better watch anyway. There's no great harm done."

"The watch is the least of it. This Esmerelda character's put ideas into Mr. Hayes' head about talkin' to his dead mother—"

Dr. Brown broke in: "—and she's got Kitty convinced she can call up her first husband. Don't worry, McCoy. I feel no threat in being rivaled by a dead man. Kitty's more than welcome to go on loving my predecessor as long as she likes." He smiled unconcernedly, and a tender expression came into his face. "Her capacity for devotion only makes her all the dearer to me."

McCoy took a deep, vexed breath: she felt Dr. Brown was missing the crux of the matter. "But the very idea of *talking* with the dead—"

Dr. Brown shook his head. "You're a nurse, McCoy. You should know that women in Kitty's condition get strange ideas."

Kitty opened the door then, looking mildly concerned. Behind her, Ken peered out and asked if Silas was alright.

Since Dr. Brown hadn't rushed off, obviously things couldn't be too dire. Still, it was natural for folks to be concerned when a nurse puts in an unexpected appearance at a doctor's private residence.

"Everything's fine," Dr. Brown assured the small group inside the house. "Nurse McCoy, why don't you come in a minute and get warmed up before you walk back home? We've got cookies, if you can wrest any of them away from those two ravenous wolves over there." He grinned and gestured towards Ken and Felix, who were standing near a huge platter of spiced molasses cookies.

McCoy followed the doctor inside. Ken frowned petulantly, broke one of the cookies in half, then broke it in half again and offered McCoy one quarter-part of the cookie with an exaggerated air of great self-sacrifice. Felix chuckled and passed McCoy the platter, then stole Ken's remaining three-fourths cookie for himself.

Kitty laughed at their performance as she sat down. Then she told McCoy she was glad to see her. "I've been thinking so much on that spiritualist we met this afternoon, Nurse McCoy." She pulled her stopped watch from her pocket and held it in her lap, tenderly caressing the fob that held her first husband's hair. "I've been wondering if you weren't too hasty in dismissing it all as humbug—"

McCoy would have interrupted her then, but she saw Dr. Brown give her a warning look over his wife's shoulder.

"—After all," Kitty went on. "There have been so many great men who believed whole-heartedly in spiritualism. Why, Mrs. Lincoln herself hired mediums to help her talk to her poor little Willie after he'd passed on."

"She might have been better served looking ahead a little and seeing what was about to happen to her husband," McCoy remarked wryly.

Kitty looked as if she'd been struck. "Oh!" She put her hand to her mouth and gazed down sadly at the watch fob.

Dr. Brown rushed to his wife's side. "Kitty, it's alright," he reassured her, putting his arms around her shoulders and petting her hair. "Don't upset yourself." He frowned over at McCoy.

Kitty sniffed, and stroked the watch fob. After a moment she looked up again, and there was a slight moisture at the corners of her eyes. She asked McCoy, "But— but, don't you *want* it all to be true? Don't you wish it could be?"

"I can wish I'd trip on a lump of gold walkin' down the street, that don't mean it's gonna happen."

"McCoy!" Dr. Brown looked at her sharply. "I'd like a word with you." He tenderly stroked his wife's cheek. "I'll be right back, Kitty." He kissed her forehead, then looked over at the pair of young men standing awkwardly in the corner. "Ken, why don't you tell Kitty about those new tricks you've been practicing on your bicycle?"

Ken brightened and launched into a description of some elaborate trick, modeling the moves as he described them and looking as if he were either wrestling or dancing with an invisible partner.

Dr. Brown drew McCoy into the rear of the little house. "Now, see here—" He told her sternly. "I don't believe in these humbugs any more than you do, but I'd rather humor my patients than upset them —especially my wife, and especially in her condition. Understood?"

"And what you propose doin' with Mr. Hayes? He ain't in no delicate condition, and this spiritualist nonsense has got him just as riled up as yer missus."

Dr. Brown sighed and shook his head. "It's all just a bunch of harmless nonsense. It'll keep him occupied until Jacob and Addie come back."

"Yeah —well, I'm just hopin' that when they do come back it won't be to find their uncle in the county insane asylum."

Dr. Brown shook his head and gave a short laugh. "I trust you won't let that happen, McCoy."

They went back out into the parlor, where Felix and Kitty were both watching Ken. He was balanced on the toes of one foot, with the other far above his head while he leaned far over with his hands on the stool of Kitty's parlor organ. "It's all just a matter of balance," he said as McCoy and Dr. Brown entered the room.

"Is that another new bike trick, Ken?" Dr. Brown asked dubiously.

Felix began saying wryly, "If he doesn't break his ne—"

Dr. Brown shot Felix an angry look and the young man realized it would be hideously poor taste to joke about broken necks in front of Kitty. Her first husband had died of a broken neck after the snake spooked his horse.

Felix amended, "That is, if he *manages* to break his noble record of botching every attempt at it."

"I just need more practice," Ken insisted, hopping back to both feet.

"I can't even exactly picture what you're trying to do, Ken," Dr. Brown admitted.

"The stool's my handlebars," Ken explained, leaning over and bracing himself on it again. "One foot on the seat, and the other back behind me in the air." He resumed his former position. "I saw a picture of it in *Illustrated Sporting and Dramatic News*."

Dr. Brown chuckled dubiously and shook his head. "Well, Ken, you know where my office is."

"Laugh while you can, folks. It's only a matter of time." Ken straightened again.

McCoy prepared to go, but Kitty stopped her. "Nurse McCoy?" Kitty frowned, then sighed and looked down. The doctor went to his wife and put an arm around her shoulders, then she looked up at Nurse McCoy again. "Even if you don't believe, will you still please let me know when Esmerelda comes back? I'd like to be there when she contacts the spirits again."

Dr. Brown smoothed his wife's hair back and smiled reassuringly at her. "We'll all be there." He looked over at Ken and Felix. "Won't we men?"

The two young chums shrugged. "Sure, Doc," Ken promised.

"I'm game," Felix agreed.

McCoy remembered Felix's profession and reflected sourly, *Well now when Mr. Hayes and Mrs. Brown make fools of themselves there'll be a reporter there —someone whose business is to stick his nose in everybody else's business, and then run and tell the paper about it before the business is even concluded.* She eyed Felix suspiciously, then re-lit her lantern and bid the company goodbye before venturing out alone into the inky night. *And here I thought talking to the doctor would help things!*

Chapter IX

The next morning when she went out to pick some mint, McCoy heard a rustling of leaves in the kitchen garden. She looked over and saw a thin, unkempt grey tabby cat rolling lazily over the flattened branches of a sizeable catnip bush.

McCoy gave the cat a stern look. "That catnip's supposed to be for treating fevers, you know. Where'd you come from, anyways?"

The cat stretched out, showing ribs through her tangled fur. Then she pushed her head backwards against the catnip, purring. Despite being malnourished (and apparently without a home), the cat seemed happy with her current position in life.

McCoy shook her head. "Bad as a drunkard!" She continued past her to the mint patch.

After she'd cut the mint for Silas' tea, the cat followed her to the kitchen with an expectant look. She slipped past her ankles right through the kitchen door, then looked around and sauntered over to the refrigerator.

McCoy glared down at her. "Well, why do you expect me to feed you?"

The cat sniffed the air, then sat up on her hind legs and pawed at the latch of the ice compartment.

McCoy shook her head. "I suppose word's gotten around that it's my lot in life to care for all the world's fools who don't have the sense to take care of themselves!"

The cat miaowed.

McCoy shook her head again. "My cross to bear, I suppose." She took a piece of beef liver out from between the blocks of ice in the refrigerator, cut off a hunk, and tossed it out into the garden for the cat. After the little animal had followed it outside, McCoy shut the door again to keep in the heat from the stove, then went back to her duties.

Silas didn't come down for breakfast at his usual time, despite having gone to bed so early the previous night. When the sun's rays grew long through the mansion's large windows and there was still no sign of him, McCoy started to become concerned. She went upstairs to his room and knocked firmly on the door. "You awake?"

Silas answered in a feeble voice, "Yes. Come in."

McCoy entered the room and found Silas seated by the big, bay view window of his room, anxiously watching the road. He was dressed to receive company, but he was very pale. McCoy didn't like that pallor —or how frail he looked. She'd spent the last four months convincing Silas he was neither so old nor so ill as he'd believed he was when she arrived, and she couldn't abide people undoing her hard work.

"Your breakfast is gettin' cold," she told him with an air of authority. "So unless you want me to keep re-heating and re-heatin' it until it ain't fit for hogs to eat—"

"I'm not hungry," Silas cut her off.

McCoy frowned. "You need to keep regular meals—"

"Bring it up here, then." Silas snapped. He turned back to the window.

McCoy squared her jaw. "Now, look here! I know you'd barely left this room for years before I come, but gettin' you to walk down those stairs for your vittles was my first step towards gettin' you to see that your ills were all in your head that whole time. I won't have you backsliding now, d'ye hear?"

Silas regarded McCoy with a chastised expression that reminder her of her father's old hound dog. "All right," he said meekly, then obediently followed her downstairs.

He was quiet as she served up his cream of rice and stewed prunes. She'd eaten her own breakfast hours before, but after pouring his mint tea for him she poured a cup for herself and sat down with him. Dr. Brown always said that Silas' only real problem was that he was lonely.

"There's a stray cat sniffing around outside," McCoy remarked conversationally.

"Oh?" Silas seemed only slightly interested.

"Don't know where it came from."

"I don't mind cats." He shrugged. "It'll keep any mice away. If it's still here when Jacob and Addie come back, he'll be glad to have it around. He likes cats." He took a slow, contemplative bite of his cream of rice. "He takes after my mother that way."

He slowly tipped his spoon into his cream of rice again, then he set the spoon down and looked nervously towards the front of the house. "Can't we sit somewhere we can look out onto the road? I'd like to watch—"

"You're frettin' yourself into more of a stew than those prunes there," McCoy pointed at the fruit. "You just finish up and I'll take you on a nice, long walk. A walk will be just the thing for you to work off all that nervous energy."

Silas nodded reluctant agreement and took up his spoon again.

Then the doorbell rang.

McCoy cursed inwardly. *If that's that Esmerelda creature, he won't even finish his breakfast now*, she thought in irritation as she watched Silas set aside his spoon. —*Let alone get the walk he needs.*

"Hurry and answer that, McCoy," Silas urged. "If it's Miss Gracilis, show her into the parlor." He drew his napkin from his lap and dropped it onto the table.

McCoy noted with displeasure that he'd barely eaten anything. The doorbell rang again and she went to answer it, though she had disapproval firmly stamped on all her features.

When she opened the door Esmerelda was standing outside in the sort of dress Rachel Goldstein would lose her head over. It overflowed with flounces and ruffles, and there was a wire basket or chicken-coop arrangement in the back of the skirt to make it have the appearance of a city lot, narrow in front but running back a good ways. McCoy reflected that at least on Rachel it would have been becoming, but on this Esmerelda it struck her as vulgar affectation.

Esmerelda regarded McCoy with that peculiar variety of haughtiness unique to the middle classes. "I've come to see Mr. Hayes," she announced with an air of great authority.

McCoy turned the full force of her disturbingly direct gaze on the woman for a moment.

You don't fool me none, you polecat in a petticoat.
"I'm sure you remember where the parlor is," she
stated flatly, letting the door swing open.

Esmerelda's eyes widened at the insolence of
the remark, then she swept past McCoy in a
thundering storm of silk.

McCoy shut the door, then went to get Silas.

"Is it Miss Gracilis?" He asked nervously.

"Yep. She's in the parlor."

Silas started to move past McCoy, but she
stopped him. "Sir?"

Silas looked at McCoy in surprise. She'd been
in his service more than four months, but this was the
first time she'd addressed him quite so politely.
"What is it, McCoy?"

"Be careful with that one. She ain't what she
makes out to be."

Silas frowned but didn't answer. McCoy
followed him into the parlor, her concern deepening.

Esmerelda was seated on a swoop-backed
divan and had arranged herself so that her skirts took
up more than half of the long seat. Her demeanor was
entirely different when she addressed Silas than it had
been when she'd spoken to McCoy at the door.
Whereas before she'd been haughty, now she was
simpering. She showed an exaggerated concern for
Silas and inquired into his health with a calculated
show of tenderness.

She's spotted his weak place already, McCoy
noted. She supposed she might have expected it: a
man who kept a trained nurse in service obviously
had preoccupations with his health. McCoy supposed
that either Kitty or Silas had mentioned her place in

the household last time Esmerelda had called, or else the spiritualist had deduced McCoy's profession from seeing her nursing chatelaine. *For all her empty-headed airs, she might be more observant than she lets on,* McCoy reflected. She re-doubled her determination to keep a sharp eye on her.

Esmerelda asked Silas about his digestion, then inquired whether he might not be worried about consumption as the damp weather was about to set in.

How does she know the exact two things he worries about most? McCoy wondered. *Lucky guess, maybe?*

Silas launched into a long dissertation on the state of his health, and Esmerelda expressed sympathy for all his imagined ills in a way that anyone besides a confirmed hypochondriac should have known was a sham.

The last thing he needs is someone humoring his ideas about being sick, McCoy thought with concern. *He's been getting better, but if he gets encouraged to believe those moans and groans of his have a reason behind them, he'll be bed-bound again by the end of the month.*

After encouraging Silas to expand on his perceived maladies for longer than was good for him, Esmerelda took a small glass bottle from her reticule. "I made this for you," she said tenderly, holding it out towards Silas. "—Under the guidance of my companion spirit. It's an elixir of health identical to the one used by the great Galen himself!"

To his credit, Silas did seem slightly doubtful about the far-fetched nature of this claim. He clearly wanted to believe, though. Whatever his doubts, it is a very rare man who can turn down a gift offered by a lovely young woman looking at him with tenderness in her eyes. He reached for the bottle.

McCoy strode over and snatched the bottle from Esmerelda's hand before Silas could take it. "Give me that!" She popped the cork out using the little corkscrew on her nursing chatelaine and sniffed suspiciously at the bottle's contents. As the fiery scent of nearly pure alcohol wafted up, she wrinkled her nose in disgust. "If this is anything like what Galen used, then the father of medicine was a moonshiner. This smells like my cousin Zeke's old still."

She pulled the stopper off her corkscrew and thrust it back into the neck of the bottle. "It ain't no different from those quack remedies peddled by the patent medicine salesmen I always send packing."

Silas looked nervously from McCoy to Esmerelda, caught between contradicting his authoritative nurse and insulting his beautiful young guest.

"Have Dr. Brown sniff it, if you don't believe me," McCoy suggested. "He'll tell you the same thing."

Esmerelda quickly grabbed the bottle from McCoy and thrust it back into her reticule. "The medicine loses its value in the presence of unbelievers," she declared as she hid it from view.

Silas eyed her questioningly.

Esmerelda saw his doubt and wisely switched tactics. "But it's really your family you'd like to discuss, isn't it?" She suggested in a soft, warm tone.

"—Your parents who've passed on, Lily and Edward?"

Silas looked astonished. "How do you know their names?"

Esmerelda smiled mysteriously. "Their spirits know who they were, before they passed over the blessed river. They still remember you with all the great love they bore you during their lives. Shall we call up their spirits together and hear their messages for you?" She reached for Silas' hands.

McCoy spoke up wryly. "Watch out for your watch, there. It's a nicer one than that Waterbury of Mrs. Brown's."

Esmerelda gave McCoy a pained look, then turned her large brown eyes on Silas with a languorous expression. "Whatever happened yesterday was the spirits' will, not my own," she told him. "I'm sure you won't be afraid of your parents' spirits?" She reached for his hands again.

"If you really must be calling up spirits," McCoy interrupted, remembering Dr. Brown's advice about humoring these queer notions. "Mrs. Brown said she wants to be here when you do it again. And the doc', too, and Mrs. Simmons' brother." She didn't mention Felix. She still didn't like the idea of a reporter witnessing all this nonsense.

Silas frowned. "Dr. Brown wants to be here?"

"Yep."

A worried look crossed Esmerelda's face. Whatever she was planning, she didn't seem to want other people present. Realizing this, McCoy decided she herself *did* want other people present, and she pressed the point.

"It'll be good to have the doctor and his wife by again —and Ken Kellam's your family now, since his sister married your nephew," McCoy told Silas. "You can't very well turn down family that wants to visit."

Silas raised his eyebrows slightly. Then a contemplative look came into his features, followed by a very discrete smile. "I suppose he is family now..." he mused quietly to himself.

Esmerelda pursed her lips. "It seems a very tenuous relation at best—"

"Family's family." McCoy cut her off.

Silas nodded slowly. "If the boy wants to be here, he's welcome. Dr. and Mrs. Brown, too." He looked at Esmerelda. "You did say you needed more people for what you're going to do. Can you come back tonight? Young Kell—" He stopped, then smiled and corrected himself. "Ken works at the shipping office so he won't be late, and Dr. Brown usually stops seeing patients around dusk. If you can be here around nightfall I'll send word for them to meet us after work."

Esmerelda smiled in a way that reminded McCoy of a cat about to eat a mouse. "Yes, actually it's better to do these things after dark. We'll need a basin of water in the seance space, and a round table big enough for all of us to sit around."

Silas looked thoughtful. "Now, I had hoped there wouldn't be any unnecessary delay but it's not so very long to wait, and my mother always said—"

"—That patience is a virtue," Esmerelda interjected.

Silas regarded her curiously. "That's right. How did you know that?"

She rose from her seat, smiling in a mysterious way. She flicked her skirts straight; the way the flounces rose, then settled reminded McCoy of a preening bird fluffing its feathers. "Oh, I know many things, Silas Benedick."

She moved towards him and for a brief moment it looked disturbingly like Esmerelda was about to pick Silas' pocket. Her hand made a complicated gesture and she produced a dried flower, seemingly out of thin air. She ran it coyly along the curve of her cheek, then handed it to Silas with a smile. She blinked slowly to show off her long eyelashes, then she turned towards McCoy in a way that showed her figure to best advantage from Silas' perspective.

She looked down at McCoy. "Will you show me out?"

McCoy would have liked to boot this hussy out with a swift kick to her bustled backside, but she held her temper and her tongue.

After she'd taken Esmerelda outside and locked the front door behind her, McCoy stomped back to the parlor. Silas was still holding the dried flower and staring at it with a dumbfounded look.

McCoy folded her arms in front of herself and cocked her head at Silas. "Are you seriously being taken in by that humbug?"

Silas looked at her. "Don't you think it's all very strange?"

"I've seen a lot of mighty strange things, but never anything that couldn't be explained by reason and good sense. When my cousin Jeb chased his neighbor's rooster two miles through the woods without slow nor pause it seemed mighty strange — until we all found out the dumbed bird had swallowed his wife's wedding ring."

Silas didn't answer. He just continued looking at the flower, and at last held it up. "Do you know what this is?"

McCoy strode over and squinted at it. "It's an asphodel, isn't it?"

He nodded. "My mother's favorite flower — and my sister's. Do you know what it means?"

"I know it's a diuretic. If you're asking about that language of flowers nonsense I never went in for that sort of thing. I leave that to gals like Mrs. Simmons."

Silas regarded the dried bloom. "It means 'Remembered beyond the tomb.'"

"Your sister's still alive," McCoy pointed out. "You can remember her all you like without tombs coming into it."

Silas frowned at the flower, then looked up at McCoy. "How did Miss Gracilis know my Christian name? Did you mention it to her?"

McCoy shook her head. "Why would I? And besides, I don't recollect ever knowing your middle name was Benedick." She squinted at Silas. "Were your parents English or something?"

Silas looked embarrassed. "No, just very avid readers of Shakespeare." He twisted the dried asphodel thoughtfully in his fingers. "I try not to let people know my middle name. I don't know how someone who's never met me before could learn it…"

McCoy didn't like the troubled look on Silas face, so she decided a distraction was in order. "How about finishing that breakfast?" She suggested. "Stewed prunes are just as good cold as hot, and then we can go out for our walk—"

"No, McCoy." Silas interrupted. "I don't really feel up to it today. And Miss Gracilis is right: I need to look after my health with the wet weather coming on."

McCoy scowled at him. "Just look outside!" She marched over to the parlor window and gestured out to where the russet foliage of big leaf maples stood out crisp as paper against a blue October sky. "I've never seen such a pretty day! Not a hint of rain anywhere, no wind to speak of —why, it's a sin against nature to stay indoors on a day like this!"

"Maybe," Silas said with a sad expression. "Maybe. But… I'm tired." He rose slowly. "I'm going to go up to my room and have a nap."

"You just got up not more than two hours ago!"

He sighed. "If you could let Dr. Brown and Ken know when to come over tonight, I'd appreciate it. Then take the rest of the day off. If you want to come back in time for tonight's gathering you can, but I know you don't put much stock in it." He turned his back on her and moved slowly towards the stairs.

Chapter X

I'll be dumbed if I leave my post while that creature gets up to who-knows-what with someone in my charge! The very idea that she'd absent herself from the evening's proceedings almost made McCoy mad enough to spit.

Back when she was a ward nurse in charge of thirty-two beds, McCoy would have considered her present job a sinecure: just one man to look after (and him not really sick), and a big, fancy bedroom to lodge in nicer than anything she'd even dreamed about as a barefoot girl in the Smoky Mountains. But the sham nature of everything she had to deal with these days was really wearing on her. Just when she thought she was getting somewhere convincing Silas all his ills were in his head and that he just needed to get out more, along comes this conjuring hussy encouraging his unhealthy notions and giving him even more far-fetched ideas. It almost made McCoy nostalgic for her old days as a ward nurse: at least then the problems she had to deal with were *real*. Maternity service, rheumatic subjects, hemorrhages… even the delirium tremens cases had a more firm reality to their symptoms than the queer goings-on she'd been dealing with in the past few days.

But she wasn't about to quit. She'd pledged long ago never to give up on a patient who needed her, and in his own strange, aggravating way, she could tell Silas needed her more than most. The real question was how to help him.

As she cleared Silas' uneaten breakfast from the dining room table, McCoy fell back on her old teacher's technique of assessing the things she knew for sure were true:

1. Silas really cared about two things in life: his family, and his health.
2. Just after Silas' nephew got married, a letter came for him signed with the initials of Silas' deceased mother, and written in a hand which seemed to be identical to hers.
3. This strange letter caused Silas to lose sleep, and predisposed him to ideas about spirits.
4. A few days after the letter arrived, Esmerelda showed up claiming she could communicate with his mother.
5. Esmerelda seemed to know the exact points of Silas' health that fretted him most. She also knew personal details like his obscure middle name.
6. Esmerelda had very nimble fingers.

McCoy frowned as she added this last detail to her mental list, remembering the trick with the flower. She had her doubts about how truly relevant this detail was to the case, but it did fall into the category of things she knew were true, so she kept it under consideration.

The only conclusion she reached after outlining things was that Esmerelda somehow had to have been involved with the sending of the letter. How the woman had managed it was a total mystery, though.

After she'd cleaned up breakfast McCoy went downtown to oblige Silas' request that she tell Dr.

Brown and Ken about the meeting to call up the spirits.

Dr. Brown was off on a house call again so she left a note on his office slate. When she went into the shipping office and asked for Ken Kellam, everyone within ear-shot of the door turned towards her in surprise.

"What is it you want with Ken?" The man who'd answered the door asked curiously.

"Just relaying a message. Could you let him know that the meeting he promised Dr. Brown he'd come to is happening up at Mr. Silas Hayes' house tonight?"

The man at the door smiled. "Sure, I'll let him know!"

"Thank you."

Peering across the room, McCoy could see Ken working diligently at a far desk. Up until now she'd mostly seen him in bicycling knickers, cracking jokes and pulling off feats of gymnastics. It was an interesting contrast to see him in his clerk's suit and smudged sleeve protectors, concentrating over long rows of figures. It suddenly occurred to her that perhaps the tedium of his office job was precisely why the spirited young man was so unrestrained in his off-hours.

He must have felt eyes on him because he looked up. Seeing McCoy at the door he gave a friendly smile and a short wave, then went back to his work.

The shipping office where Ken worked wasn't far from the newspaper office; McCoy considered going there and telling Felix about the seance. Dr.

Brown had wanted Felix to come, even if McCoy had neglected to mention that detail to Silas. Then, too, the Simmonses almost fell under McCoy's sphere of responsibility (after all, Addie Simmons had been McCoy's patient for a short while), and they were fond of Felix. Addie seemed to consider him in the light of an adopted brother.

But the fact remained that he was a reporter. McCoy still didn't like the idea of a reporter meddling in the affairs of one of her patients. There was just far too much potential for mischief. Besides, he'd done something mighty strange on the day Jacob and Addie got married, and she still hadn't heard an explanation for it.

She'd watched Jacob and Silas go off to the wedding, and she was absolutely sure she'd locked the front door when she came back inside the house. But, just as she was finishing washing up the breakfast dishes she'd heard that same front door burst open with a bang and someone tore up the stairs like the devil himself was on his heels. Alarmed at the commotion, McCoy rushed out of the kitchen armed with a cast iron frying pan, determined to put up a good fight if some sort of threat had invaded. She was astonished to see Felix Halloway, of all people, come racing back down the stairs three at a time, jacket off and covered in sweat. He didn't pause to explain himself but ran straight out the door again, leaving it swinging behind him. Afterwards McCoy asked Silas about the incident, but he'd been as puzzled as she was.

McCoy chewed the memory over in her mind as she walked up to the newspaper office. She frowned at the door, then turned and went back towards Silas' house without further pause.

Chapter XI

Ken must have told Felix about the meeting, because the two chums arrived together before the Browns or Esmerelda showed up. McCoy lured Ken into the kitchen with an offer of cornbread and told him to eat all he wanted. As soon as he seemed preoccupied, McCoy pulled Felix aside and into the dining room.

"I'll tell you right now I don't like you being here!" She informed him bluntly, looking him straight in the eyes.

Felix looked shocked —and hurt. "What did I—"

McCoy cut him off. "I don't hold with newspaper reporters. Y'all are meddlesome, and as a general rule, inclined to tellin' whoppers my six-year-old niece would know better than to believe. And furthermore, I am by general inclination opposed to givin' away the family secrets of the folks I care for, or to lettin' other folks ferret 'em out!"

Understanding dawned on Felix's face, then he pressed his lips together, looked down, and nodded. "Well, ma'am," he said then, looking back up at McCoy. "When it comes to most men in my profession, I agree with you."

McCoy's jaw dropped and she stared at him.

He went on, "Certainly that's the type of thing my editor prefers. If I went in for that sort of yellow journalism I might actually have my own desk by now, instead of sharing space with two junior reporters at the office standing desk and mostly writing my pieces away from the office altogether."

He sighed and shook his head. "But the fact of the matter is, I've made it my life's goal to purify and ennoble journalism. I'm sure it sounds naive — actually, to tell the truth, Nurse McCoy, there are plenty of days when I myself think it's naive, but it's a goal I refuse to lose sight of. It'd rather lose my job than write a single word that wasn't true, and I'll churn out fluff pieces before I expose any secrets to the light of day that don't full well deserve exposure. I only investigate things when I think writing about them will help clean up this dirty old world we live in."

McCoy squinted at him suspiciously. He seemed to honestly believe what he was saying, but she had her doubts. "Am I truly supposed to believe that?" She asked. "You reporters ain't got no sort of accountability —most of the time y'all don't even sign your real names to those articles you write!"

Felix brightened and gave a short laugh. "You mean our writing handles?"

"I mean those silly nicknames you hide behind—"

Felix shrugged, regaining some of his usual easy-going demeanor. "That's just convention. I'm happy to tell you my handle —I'm Spark."

The byline seemed familiar: McCoy frowned, trying to remember which articles she'd seen it paired with. She had a vague recollection that she'd approved of them.

After concentrating a moment, her memory provided an example. "Say," she ventured. "Ain't you the one who wrote all them pieces about the dog-fighting ring with all that gambling down on the waterfront? And you finally got the sheriff to move his bones and do somethin' about it?"

Felix grinned in a slightly embarrassed way. "Yeah, that was me."

Ken came through the kitchen door into the dining room carrying two large pieces of cornbread, one slightly bigger than the other. He'd apparently heard at least the last part of McCoy and Felix's conversation. He added, "Felix made sure all those dogs got to decent people afterwards, too."

Ken handed Felix the bigger piece of cornbread and went on, "The most vicious ones actually turned out to be pretty good hunting dogs for men 'way out of town, and a lot of the weaker pups got turned into family pets." He gave Felix a friendly punch in the arm and added in an aside to him, "Too bad about that bulldog."

McCoy looked at them questioningly.

Felix explained, "There was a bulldog I got pretty attached to —the best bulldog I'd ever seen. I'd have liked to take him in myself, but the room I rent is barely big enough for my bike and me. I can live there, but I wouldn't make a dog do it."

"So he gave him to the butcher!" Ken broke in with a grin. "Now that dog probably gets to eat more meat than you do, Spark!"

Felix shrugged philosophically. "Ah, well..." He held up his cornbread. "I can't complain." He took a large bite.

McCoy squinted at him a moment while he ate, wondering if she'd been assuming too much and if he might be a decent sort after all. "And what about that business last week?" She asked. "—When you came tearing through here like a 'coon chased by hounds? What was all that about?"

Felix and Ken both looked surprised, then they chuckled softly. Felix shook his head. "You're gonna have to ask Jacob about the details of that one. It's up to him whether he wants word getting around or not. I don't give out my friends' secrets."

"I'll tell ya!" Ken volunteered with a mischievous grin. "Jacob for—"

Felix clapped a hand over Ken's mouth. "And you'll keep mum about it, too!" He warned in a jocular way. "—Unless you want to go hunting for your steering grips in your wood pile." He mussed his chum's hair, then let him go.

Ken grinned back, shrugging and combing his hair back into place with his fingers. "Have it your way!"

McCoy eyed Felix and sucked at the corner of her mouth. After some consideration she told him, "You're alright, you know that?"

"Thanks." He smiled in a self-deprecating way. Then he grinned. "Does that mean I get more corn bread?"

Chapter XII

When the Browns arrived McCoy tapped on Silas' door and let him know all his guests were downstairs.

"Does that include Miss Gracilis?" He asked nervously as he came out.

"I don't count her as a guest."

He sighed. "Let's go down. Bring a basin from one of the guest rooms down with us —Miss Gracilis said she needed a basin of water."

After greeting his guests Silas asked Ken and Felix if they'd mind moving some chairs and a round table from the dining room into the parlor. As they obliged him, Silas went to speak with the Browns.

McCoy frowned over Kitty's morbid choice of dress for the evening. She was wearing full mourning. Kitty had been the town dressmaker before she married the doctor and McCoy knew she had plenty of lovely gowns back home, but the somber black dress covering her form tonight was old and worn. Judging from the slightly darker black at the seams, it looked very likely to have been dyed as a fully completed dress, rather than made from black fabric to begin with. McCoy felt fairly certain it was Kitty's wedding dress from her marriage to her first husband, dyed black for mourning when he passed away. The only ornament which broke up the somberness of the attire was the hair locket watch fob, now worn on a black ribbon around her neck.

Kitty and Silas soon absorbed themselves in nervous speculation about how the evening would proceed. Noticing McCoy's scrutiny of his wife, Dr.

Brown pulled the nurse aside. "I'll admit I'm a little worried too," he confided, agreeing with McCoy before she'd even voiced her opinion. "I didn't expect Kitty to take this quite so seriously."

"It ain't healthy," McCoy told him. "Ain't healthy for anyone to carry on like that, and especially in her condition—"

"I know." Dr. Brown frowned and took a deep breath. "But I'm afraid it would only make things worse if I try to argue the point and upset her. At least now she's fairly happy, even if she is also slightly nervous."

McCoy frowned, glancing over to where Kitty was talking with Silas. Her voice was high-pitched and she was fidgeting. He was even more quiet than usual, and kept glancing towards the door. "He's nervous, too." McCoy told Dr. Brown. "I don't like it. As far as I'm concerned, the sooner all this is over, the better."

"I'm in agreement with you there. I'm hoping that after tonight they'll have both worked all this out of their systems."

"I wouldn't be so sure about that, Doc'."

The doorbell rang and Silas looked towards the front of the house with eager eyes. "Show her into the parlor," he told McCoy.

"You know," she protested, folding her arms across her chest. "Answering doors really isn't part of my nursing duties."

Her actual nursing duties for Silas were so light, when she'd come here she'd taken to answering the door voluntarily —but that was when she thought there might actually be someone on the other side who could benefit her patient.

Silas looked surprised at this sudden deviation in routine but after only the slightest hesitation he agreed with her. "You're right, of course. It's not part of our contract." He went to answer the door himself.

And it's ridiculous for the owner of a place like this to be answering his own door, McCoy reflected. She couldn't wait until Addie Simmons took up her role as lady of the house and finally added some sense of order to the place.

Dr. Brown went back to his wife in front of the parlor door and McCoy retrieved Ken and Felix from down the hall by the dining room.

Esmerelda entered with Silas. She was wearing a long cloak that covered her almost to the floor and she had a sort of cinnamon-rose blush on her cheeks. McCoy was morally certain it was a sham blush, as it was permanent, and was a little nearer to her left ear than to her right one.

As they covered the short distance from the front door to the door of the parlor, McCoy could see that Esmerelda's behavior towards Silas had changed significantly since she'd first arrived at the house the day before, announced by her scandalous brochure. At that first meeting Esmerelda had been polite and smiling with Silas, but now something else had entered her demeanor —something unseemly that McCoy didn't like one little bit.

Silas was old enough to be Esmerelda's father, but she was making eyes at him like a schoolgirl regarding her swain. To his credit he seemed more confused about it than anything, but despite his innocence in the matter McCoy still **Did Not Like** this state of affairs.

Esmerelda stopped in front of the parlor door. "I need some time to prepare," she told Silas in a soft voice, laying a hand familiarly over his heart. He frowned down at it in surprise. "In order to call up those who have gone before—" Esmerelda continued, "I must first commune with my spirit guide."

Silas stared confusedly at her hand resting on his chest. "Er..." he stammered uneasily. "Take all the time you need."

She moved into the parlor with a sensual rippling of her long cloak and shut the door behind her. Silas seemed more confused than ever.

Ken sniggered. "I think she's sweet on you, Uncle Silas."

Felix looked around at the richly furnished mansion and remarked wryly, "Yeah, she's sweet on something..."

Silas scowled. "Don't be ridiculous, you two. She's only here because I asked—" He paused. "What was that you called me, Ken?"

"Uncle Silas? I just figured that since my sister married your nephew—"

Silas nodded. "I'm glad you feel that way," he told Ken, then he smiled. "It's good to have more family."

Out of the corner of her eye McCoy could see an approving expression on Dr. Brown's face.

After a time they heard a faint tinkling music coming from the parlor. They looked at each other in surprise, then Silas tapped lightly on the door. From the other side, Esmerelda called out in a slow, sing-song voice, "Enter!"

The assembled company looked at each other questioningly then Silas (being the closest) opened the door. A powerful wave of patchouly came flooding out of the parlor.

Ken wrinkled his nose in distaste. "Pee-ew!" He remarked in a quiet aside to Felix, "Smells like someone just unloaded a whole shipment of India shawls!"

Esmerelda had turned out all the lamps —the ones in wall-mounted sconces as well as the large ones on tables. The parlor remained lit only by a single candle. The round table Ken and Felix had moved from the dining room was now covered with the long cloak Esmerelda had been wearing when she'd come in, and the candle shared central space there with the basin of water. Small pieces of lined paper were arranged around these two objects. On the far side of the table sat Esmerelda.

She was in a thin muslin dress cut in a style that would have been shockingly low even for a ball gown. Three long necklaces of beads hung heavy on the dress' plunging neckline and pulled it even lower than it would have been on its own. She wore thick gold earrings and had unpinned her hair. The light brown tresses flowed in rippling waves down her back. The overall effect was like a modern portrayal of a sorceress in one of the medieval stories Jacob and Addie were always reading.

McCoy wanted to march over and wrangle the hussy out the door right then and there. Dr. Brown saw the agitation she was about to start and motioned for her to control herself. She managed it, but it took effort.

Ken and Felix went in first. They were unfazed by the eerie atmosphere and entered with their usual easy-going strides. Silas followed them, regarding Esmerelda with a look between fear and awe.

Kitty held back, frightened. Dr. Brown put an arm around her shoulders. "We don't have to do this, Kitty." He sounded like he hoped she would change her mind.

Kitty bit her lip and raised her chin up a little higher. "I want to do it," she told him. She took a deep breath and entered the room, her husband at her side.

McCoy followed them and shut the door behind herself.

Silas was already seated at Esmerelda's right; Kitty took the seat at her left. Dr. Brown sat beside his wife. Next was Felix, then Ken. McCoy took the last available seat, between Ken and Silas.

The eerie, tinkling music still played on from some hidden music box. McCoy reflected that Esmerelda must have brought it in hidden underneath the long cloak she'd been wearing, and wondered where she'd secreted it. With the room so dimly lit, it could be anywhere.

The music box wound down and silence fell over the room. Esmerelda let it stretch on a long moment. Just as McCoy sensed that Ken was about to start fidgeting Esmerelda announced, "Each of you must take up the paper which lies before you."

They did so.

She went on: "Write the names of six persons. They may be real or fictitious, it matters not, but somewhere in amongst them write the name of one you wish to contact who has passed beyond the spirit river."

McCoy picked up her pencil and tried to think of six names, one of them dead.

Esmerelda kept talking incessantly. "Take up your pencils, and write six names. Be sure to use the names of living people I cannot possibly know, or fictitious names out of your own imagination. In amongst them somewhere, list the name of the one who has passed, the one you wish to contact..."

McCoy wished Esmerelda would hush up and let her concentrate. She started listing the names of her family back in Tennessee.

Esmerelda continued to drone on. After McCoy had written out the names of her father and mother, the medium exclaimed, "Now, if there are any doubters be fair with me! Be sure to include the name of one —and only one— person who has passed on. And write quickly!"

McCoy hurried to write the name of her dead grandmother, then followed it with the names of her three brothers.

When they had all finished writing Esmerelda asked them to pass their papers to her. She laid them in a stack facedown in front of herself, then lifted the top paper. She manipulated it theatrically, but it seemed to McCoy that she couldn't possibly have taken time to read all six names. Her gestures finished with both her hands (and the paper) in her lap under the table. She turned her eyes upwards and called out, "Lily Hayes!"

Silas sat up straighter.

Esmerelda dropped the paper into the water. It grew damp, then burst into flames. Most of the company gasped in surprise, but Felix simply raised an eyebrow and leaned back in his chair.

When the flame had died away there was another paper in Esmerelda's hand. Again, she didn't seem to read it but called out, "Adam Butler!"

Kitty's hand flew to her mouth and she suppressed a soft cry.

Dr. Brown leaned towards her anxiously. "Kitty, are you alright?" He whispered.

"We must be silent," Esmerelda stated. "—Lest the spirits flee!"

Kitty looked scared and quickly motioned her husband to quiet.

Esmerelda dropped the paper into the water as she had done with its predecessor, and it too burst into flame.

Dr. Brown frowned and put a protective arm around his wife's shoulders, watching her in concern. When Esmerelda announced another name his head jerked to face the medium and he frowned.

Again, water set the paper on fire. The next name Esmerelda called out was McCoy's grandmother.

How the devil did she pick out the right name, with all those others? And she's barely even looking at the papers!

The only person at the table who didn't show the slightest surprise at any of the performance was

Felix. He remained leaning back in his chair, arms folded casually across his chest. When Esmerelda lifted the last paper and called out a name, Felix's only action was to smile slightly.

After the last paper had burnt, Esmerelda covered the basin with a cloth and asked Kitty to move it from the table to the floor. She obeyed in silent reverence.

When Kitty regained her seat Esmerelda proclaimed, "The spirits thus are assembled. Let us join hands and hear their messages."

Everyone in the room took hold their neighbors' hands.

"Place your hands upon the table," Esmerelda commanded.

They did so, sitting their with their clasped hands in full view in the candlelight.

"Now," Esmerelda cast her eyes skywards. "We call upon the spirit of Lily Hayes!"

Suddenly a muffled rapping sounded in the room, as if someone had knocked on the table. McCoy instantly looked over at Esmerelda's hands, but they were still clasped by Silas on her right and Kitty on her left. McCoy kept an unwavering eye on those hands, but they did not move.

"She is here, and awaits your communication," Esmerelda stated, looking towards Silas.

Silas asked nervously, "Was it really her who sent the letter?"

The rapping sounded once again. Esmerelda's hands still did not move.

She answered Silas question solemnly, "Yes."

McCoy sensed Silas shiver slightly. To herself she reflected, *I knew this Esmerelda creature was behind that letter somehow! But how did she copy his mother's handwriting?*

Silas asked, "Why did she send it?"

A more complicated series of raps followed. McCoy still kept an eagle eye on Esmerelda's hands, but they never moved.

After the raps fell silent, Esmerelda reported, "She says that it was to announce my presence, so that with my help she could communicate with you."

Silas clearly wanted to believe, but his old lawyer instincts asserted themselves. "You'll have to provide evidence. Surely if it's my mother's spirit making those rappings she can tell you how she and my father died."

More raps, then Esmerelda reported: "Your father Edward died of cancer of the stomach. You rushed back to New York as soon as you learned of his illness, but you didn't quite make it there in time." More raps. "Your mother Lily had insisted on nursing him herself, and wore herself out with the effort. In her weakened state she contracted consumption, and that was what killed her. You stayed with your mother until the very end. Her last words were, 'Take care of Ann.'"

All the color drained from Silas' face during this speech.

Esmerelda went on, "Your mother sends her deepest love. She must go now to make way for the other spirits we have called."

Suddenly the candle went out and the room was plunged in total darkness.

A frisson of uncomfortable surprise ran around the table. Esmerelda called out, "Don't be alarmed! This is a sign that one of the other spirits we called wishes to materialize and be seen by us! Place your hands upon the table."

More rappings sounded. They were much louder this time, and they made the table reverberate. McCoy felt quite certain that if Esmerelda's hands had still been visible, this time everyone would have seen them move. But the room was completely black.

There was a long moment of inky silence. Finally, a queer-looking, vapory, luminous form emerged off to one side of the table.

There were gasps from Silas and Kitty, but McCoy heard Ken chuckle quietly to himself. She sensed a movement in the darkness as he stood. He made some sort of movement towards the glowing form.

There was a slight scuffle of some sort and the vapor suddenly agitated wildly, then shrank into nothingness and vanished. Kitty gave out a disappointed cry.

Esmerelda declared in a faint, weak voice, "I have received a great shock, and cannot proceed."

Dr. Brown ordered, "Nurse McCoy, light a lamp!"

"No!" Esmerelda cried out at the same moment McCoy stood up. "No lights!"

Doesn't want lights, eh? McCoy grabbed at the vesta on her chatelaine and quickly pulled out a match.

Dr. Brown insisted, "If there's something wrong—"

McCoy struck the match on the ridged edge of her vesta and light flared in the black room.

As the sulfur ignited everyone's eyes adjusted from total darkness to initial bright flash, then to pinprick of light as the flame consumed the sulfur and McCoy was left holding a tiny splinter of burning wood. She moved to re-light the candle, but had to do it carefully so that the motion wouldn't blow out the match.

Esmerelda slumped down on the table. "Leave me alone!"

Dr. Brown moved to feel her pulse.

"Leave me alone, all of you!" She wailed, swatting his hand away.

McCoy got the candle lighted then strode quickly to the nearest lamp.

"The spirits are disturbed!" Esmerelda cried. "They've been offended by an unbeliever and I need some time alone to calm them!"

"Let's get out of the room," Silas suggested. "Give her some time."

Dr. Brown would have examined the prostrate woman but his wife pulled him away with urgent insistence. Seeing this, McCoy stepped towards Esmerelda.

"Leave her alone, McCoy," Silas ordered.

"I'm a nurse!"

"It's not a physical matter," Esmerelda moaned weakly.

"Come out with the rest of us," Silas ordered McCoy, drawing her to the door with him.

After they'd all exited into the hallway and shut the parlor door, Ken looked around impishly. "Well, that's all gone to smash, hasn't it?"

Dr. Brown eyed him the way a father might regard a boy caught soaping the neighbor's windows. "What were you doing back there, Ken?"

"Grabbing for the pole, of course."

"*What*?!" The assembled company (all except Felix) gaped at Ken in astonishment. "What do you mean?"

Ken shrugged casually. "The pole that veil was attached to."

Kitty grew very pale. "Veil?" She asked in a stricken tone. She stared at him. "Ken, what do you mean?"

"That silk veil with luminous powder on it that she was waving around in there." Ken was still grinning when he started to say this, but when he saw the effects his words had on Kitty his cheerful expression faded. "Couldn't you tell that was just a piece of silk?" He asked gently.

Kitty grew deathly still. Tears seeped into her eyes, then she slowly told the young man, "I think you're wicked, Kenneth Kellam." A sob caught in her throat before she added, "And a dreadful liar!"

She turned and ran out through the front door.

"Kitty!" Dr. Brown rushed after his wife, pausing only to grab her wrapper from the coat tree by the door.

Silas hesitated, then followed the Browns.

Seeing him heading into the chill October night, McCoy strode after him. "Your overcoat!" She protested.

He motioned her to stay inside and took a heavy coat from the rack before leaving.

McCoy frowned and turned back to the two remaining guests.

Felix shook his head at Ken. "You could have used a little more tact in telling her that, Tanglefoot. Kitty actually believed that whole humbug was real. She honestly thought she was going to see her first husband again."

Ken hung his head like a chastised schoolboy, clearly affected by his friend's disapproval. "I had no idea she'd take it so hard," he responded meekly.

McCoy decided they were all too close to the parlor door to converse freely. Esmerelda was still in there, and she might hear them through the thin sliding door.

McCoy pulled the two young men down the hallway, almost into the kitchen, and dropped her voice. "What was it you were saying about a silk veil?"

"Couldn't you tell by the way it moved and floated?" Ken looked down regretfully. "Kitty used to be a dressmaker —I thought she of all people would recognize a piece of silk being waved around."

"She didn't want to, Ken." Felix told him. "She *wanted* to believe it was a spirit materializing, so that's what she saw."

McCoy considered, then slowly nodded. "You're both right," she agreed. "How'd Esmerelda get it to disappear like that?"

Ken shrugged. "Wadded it up real quick then shoved it under the table, maybe. That's how I'd have done it."

"More likely under her skirt," McCoy told him, considering. "Of course you're a man and wouldn't think about that. All our legs were under the table so we might have noticed if she'd shoved something there real quick."

Ken shrugged and nodded agreement, seeing the sense in this argument.

"Now," McCoy went on, "—what was it you were saying about luminous powder?"

Ken shrugged. "If she'd just used luminous paint the fabric would have been too stiff to act like that. But you can make luminous paint into powder by mixing it with turpentine and spreading it on cloth. When it dries you just shake the powder out. It never stops smelling like turpentine, though. That's probably why she drenched everything in patchouly —to mask the smell."

McCoy frowned. "I'm a nurse, not an artist. What's luminous paint?"

Again, Ken shrugged. "Just what it sounds like— paint that glows in the dark. Haven't you ever seen it?"

McCoy shook her head.

"Well, I suppose it *was* only invented a few years ago, but there's been so much talk about it in the merchant marine world I guess I assumed everyone knew about it. They're starting to paint it on life buoys so that if a man falls overboard in the dark he can be rescued easily. They're using it on moorage buoys, too —even divers are starting to use it. The clerks in the shipping office got hold of an extra jar a couple months ago and we were playing around with it: that's how I figured out the trick with the turpentine." He looked towards the door. "I hope Kitty's alright. Do you think I should go apologize to her?"

Felix shook his head. "I think you've done enough damage for one night, Tanglefoot. Try apologizing tomorrow, after she calms down."

The front door opened and Silas came back in the house. "The Browns have gone home," he explained. "I tried to make Dr. Brown come back for his overcoat, but he was too worried about his wife."

McCoy thought of Kitty's condition and looked at Silas in alarm. "Is she alright? Does Dr. Brown need my help with her?"

"She's just upset. He said she'll be fine after some rest."

She remained slightly concerned. Town folks had always struck McCoy as delicate compared to her own sturdy kin back in the Appalachians, and Kitty was in a particularly vulnerable state right now. Still, her husband was a doctor —a good one, too. McCoy supposed they'd be alright, even without her help.

Felix volunteered, "I'll drop off Doc's coat at his house. I have to go past there anyways to get back to my room downtown."

Silas nodded approval of this plan and Felix went down the hall towards the coat rack. As he was passing the parlor door it slid open.

Felix stepped aside and Esmerelda emerged into the hall. She was again wearing the long, dark cloak, and her countenance bore an air of tragic exhaustion.

Felix gave her the sort of conciliatory smile he might have offered a decent rival he'd just beaten at a sporting event. "It wasn't a bad show," he told her sympathetically. "You were doing alright until Ken stepped in things. I thought the rappings were excellent —how'd you manage them?"

Esmerelda raised her head. "The rappings come from the spirits themselves!"

Felix grinned wryly. "Oh, come on, now—"

"Felix," Silas interrupted. "Don't argue with her."

Felix's brows knit together in a surprised frown. "You don't actually believe all this humbug, do you? Just let Nurse McCoy search under her dress and find that luminous silk—"

Immediately seeing the sense in this suggestion, McCoy strode towards Esmerelda.

Esmerelda blanched.

Silas called out, "She will do no such thing! McCoy, don't go any closer to her!"

McCoy turned back towards her employer. "I am a trained nurse, after all—"

"Leave her alone!"

McCoy glowered at Silas but didn't approach any closer to the other woman.

Silas walked uneasily down the hallway. "I'm very sorry for how people have behaved tonight." He apologized nervously. "There's clearly something… interesting at work here, and I'd like to know more. Could you come back tomorrow?"

McCoy gaped at him. "Mr. Hayes! She's nothing but a—"

"McCoy!" He snapped. "You're out of line."

McCoy squared her jaw and felt her blood boil.

Esmerelda shot her a gloating look of triumph that went unnoticed by Silas. Then she quickly resumed her mask of tragic exhaustion.

She stepped towards Silas with a familiar expression that startled him. He tried to back away but ran into the wall. She laid her hand over his heart and smiled up at him; he looked down at her in mild terror. "Until tomorrow, then!" She told him in a tone so saccharine McCoy half-expected it to put the man into diabetic coma.

"Er..." He stared down at the inappropriately familiar hand. "Um, yes, tomorrow. Would you like Felix or Ken to walk you back to wherever you're staying?" He cast a pleading look down the hallway towards Ken, who raised a hand over his mouth and struggled to give the impression that he was *not* fighting barely suppressed laughter.

"Oh, no. The spirits will look after me." Esmerelda assured Silas. She slowly moved to the door and cast one long, languorous look back at him before exiting.

After she'd gone, Silas gulped and let out a sigh of relief.

Ken burst out laughing. "I told you so, Uncle Silas!"

Felix pointedly inspected an expensive silver candlestick. "Like I said, she's sweet on something around here."

Silas frowned. "I don't— You—" He stopped and shook his head, confused. At last he said, "Thank you both for coming tonight. McCoy, will you please lock the door after they leave?"

Without waiting for an answer, he shook his head again and went upstairs to his room.

McCoy shook her head and frowned as she watched him go.

Chapter XIII

After Ken and Felix left together, McCoy marched into Silas' room and went right in without knocking. As she burst through the door she demanded, "Do you mind tellin' me what in the Sam Hill you were thinking, inviting that creature back again tomorrow?"

Silas was sitting in his usual armchair by the window. He looked up at McCoy's thunderstorm entrance, but didn't have a chance to respond before she went on, "She ain't nothin' but a charlatan, and if you think I'm gonna sit by while a creature like that takes advantage of a patient in my charge—"

"Hettie?"

McCoy paused for breath.

"She knew my mother's final words, Hettie."

McCoy frowned.

Silas took a deep breath and went on: "Everything she said about the way my parents died was just as she described. Every single detail."

McCoy regarded Silas in the lamplight. He honestly wasn't much past middle age; he just usually acted so prematurely ancient that his behavior made everyone think of him as older than he was. Tonight though, he really did look old.

She pulled her chair over and sat down next to him. "How could she know that?"

He shook his head. "I don't know." He took a deep breath and looked out the window into the dark for a long moment. "I can't think of any possible way. It wouldn't be hard to learn Mrs. Brown's first husband's name —the whole town knew her as Mrs.

Butler for years, anyone might have mentioned it. I can even think of people who might have told how I rushed off to New York when I heard my father was dying. But my mother's final words? How could she possibly know that? Everyone in the room was close family, and that's not the kind of thing people talk about with strangers afterwards." He cupped his chin in his hand and stared out the window at the dark waters of Puget Sound in the distance.

"What about that silly sham with the piece of glowing silk? Doesn't that show the whole business is crooked?"

He shook his head. "No, it doesn't. Ken didn't actually catch whatever that was. Even if he had, it wouldn't explain the rest of it."

McCoy remembered being taken aback when Esmerelda had so easily picked out her dead grandmother's name from the six she had written.

Silas asked, "How does water set something on fire? And the rappings— how do you explain those knocking sounds, when her hands didn't move? And the letter… His voice trailed off.

"Silas, I'm downright sure this Esmerelda's behind that queer letter that upset you so bad."

"It was in my mother's handwriting, Hettie!"

McCoy said nothing. She couldn't admit that she'd already discovered this.

There was silence in the room a long moment. Finally, McCoy offered, "Let me fix you some warm milk. It'll calm you down." She started to move towards the door.

"Don't leave me!" He pleaded suddenly. "Please? I don't want to be alone."

McCoy nodded slowly and sat back down next to him. "Let me check your pulse."

He obediently gave her his wrist and she sat holding it gently for a long time until his heart rate calmed.

As she set his wrist down, very soft steps sounded in the quiet room. McCoy looked over and saw that the stray cat she'd met earlier had slipped into the house when so many people had been coming and going through the front door. "I guess we've got another guest," she commented casually.

Silas looked over and noticed the bedraggled little animal. McCoy saw a very faint upward twitch at one corner of his mouth. "Let her stay," he said quietly. "I don't mind cats."

McCoy leaned over and held out a hand. The cat approached, sniffed her fingers, then rubbed against her skirt. McCoy picked her up and carefully placed her in Silas' lap, petting her a bit so she would settle there. "She'll keep you warm," she suggested. "It's chilly tonight."

She turned down the covers of Silas' bed, then crossed to the door of her own room. "Try to get some good rest tonight," she advised. "I'm sure things won't seem so strange after a decent night's sleep. Things are always clearer in the daylight, anyway."

He ran his hand over the cat's bony back and the animal started to purr. He looked over at McCoy and smiled very faintly. "Thank you, Hettie."

"The name's McCoy," she reminded him. "And I'm just doing my job."

She passed through the door to her room.

Chapter XIV

Esmerelda came the next day after lunch and stayed well into the evening. Silas sent McCoy out of the room early in their interview; the length of time they spent alone together in the parlor only deepened McCoy's already profound conviction that the woman was up to no good. Even if she set aside Esmerelda's ridiculous claims about supernatural powers, McCoy was certain that Felix had hit the nail right on the head when he'd suggested that Esmerelda was suddenly showering Silas with so much attention because she was sweet on his money, and not on the man himself.

If she was a more common sort I'd start counting the silver, McCoy reflected, remembering the way Esmerelda had assessed the contents of the stately house with her first quick glance. *But that ain't her style. Nope, she's in it for all or nothing. She won't quit until he's either married her or blundered himself into a position where she can sue him for breach of promise.*

One of McCoy's cousins had been threatened with a suit for breach of promise to marry just the year before. The whole McCoy family knew that Cousin Danny was so bashful around women that he once gulped down a cup of coffee with three heaping spoonfuls of salt in it because he'd been to shy to tell his hostess that she'd mixed up the salt and sugar when she left off her spectacles. When Danny took the train to the state fair dressed in his Sunday best, a woman plunked down in the seat next to him and proceeded to chatter about "the dangers which ever beset the unmarried lady, especially the unsophisticated maiden, far, far from her native village." Danny expressed some conventional words of sympathy and the woman, taking this for encouragement, then pumped him pretty dry of facts about himself. He was too bashful to admit he was just a poor hog farmer and figured there wouldn't be much harm in making out his position in life was a little better than it was. Next thing he knew, the woman was fawning all over him and telling him he was just the protector she needed. Poor Danny had always been too bashful to contradict anything a woman said to him, and he got so flummoxed by the brazen way she tried to drape herself over his seat that he slipped off the train at the next station and never even got to see the fair. About four days later a large, long yellow envelope arrived for Danny: it was a notice from a lawyer informing him that the woman from the train was suing him for $1,200 for breach of promise to marry. The letter went on to say that if he immediately sent her a check for $1,000 she would avoid the publicity of dragging it through the courts.

Everyone knew it was well-night impossible for a man to disprove a breach of promise suit once a woman had set her claws in him, and Danny (who'd never seen a thousand dollars in his life) all but concluded that the only way out of the situation was to marry the woman, although the idea of life with such a creature downright terrified him. Fortunately for him, one of the other McCoy cousins did some digging and found that the woman in question not only had three other breach of promise schemes running, she also had just about the only thing that could be used against her to defeat the claim: a living husband. Since it was patently illegal (not to mention illogical) for a married woman to pursue a breach of promise claim the matter was dropped.

Danny had been lucky, but Nurse McCoy felt that Silas was in a far more vulnerable position. Silas really did have money, and it couldn't be expected that Esmerelda had a convenient husband lurking somewhere in the background to disprove any claims she might make. *She's all the more dangerous because the man was already in a marrying mood before this creature came*, McCoy reflected, remembering his awkward hints and questions about whether McCoy herself might be interested in the proposition. The fact that he'd asked her —plain as a mud fence and blunt as a butter-knife Hettie McCoy— about marriage testified how desperately lonely the man was. Esmerelda was young and pretty, and had demonstrated an obvious knack for telling folks things they wanted to hear.

The longer Silas and Esmerelda stayed in the parlor together, the more worried McCoy got.

When suppertime approached McCoy was glad for the opportunity of ending whatever was going on. She made beef tea and Silas' favorite panada, then used her nursing prerogative of opening a door without knocking and walked straight into the parlor.

Two of the room's velvet-upholstered chairs had been pulled very close together in front of the tiled fireplace. Esmerelda was holding Silas' right hand in both of hers and peering intently at his palm, saying, "—and we can see by the way your life line curves onto the mount of Venus that your future holds—"

"Supper!" McCoy interrupted, glaring at Esmerelda. "Supper's ready!"

Silas looked embarrassed and pulled his hand away from Esmerelda's grasp. He glanced at the clock, then looked at McCoy in a nervous, guilty way that reminded her of a dog caught eyeing the chickens. "Of course," he told her, then turned to Esmerelda. "I'm sorry, I'm afraid the rest of this will have to wait until tomorrow."

Tomorrow?! McCoy scowled. *Coming back already tomorrow?! This hussy doesn't waste any time, does she?*

"Tomorrow, then," Esmerelda agreed, rising and giving Silas a sultry look that caused him to fidget and made McCoy's blood boil.

Silas stood up from his chair. "McCoy, will you please show Miss Gracilis—"

"I ain't no parlor maid, you know," McCoy interrupted. "It ain't my responsibility to be fetchin' able-bodied people back and forth as if they didn't have the sense to find their own way to the door."

"I'll show myself out," Miss Gracilis said softly, making sure Silas could see her face as she gave McCoy a wounded look. She passed out of the room, shutting the parlor door behind her.

McCoy confronted Silas. "Just what were the two of you doin' in here together all afternoon?"

"Talking," he answered meekly.

"Talking?" McCoy repeated suspiciously. "I ain't never managed to get more'n an hour's conversation outta you on any subject 'ceptin' your bowels, and I doubt you were talkin' on them all that time!"

"No," Silas admitted. "Miss Gracilis did most of the talking. She knows a remarkable amount about me, McCoy. She was even able to remind me of things I'd half-forgotten myself."

"Like what?"

"Like the title of the last book my mother ever read, and advice I gave Jacob on chess strategy when he and I sat with my mother during her last illness." He looked intently at McCoy. "How could she possibly know those sorts of details, unless there really is something to her claims about conversing with spirits?"

McCoy's brow furrowed. "I don't know," she admitted. "But I'm determined to find out."

She could tell that Silas' nerves were in a wrought-up state and she hadn't helped by agitating him further. She opened the parlor door gently, the quiet way she'd been taught in nursing school, and left into the hallway.

Despite her earlier protest, McCoy knew of course that the real reason for showing people to the door was to lock it after they left. Since Esmerelda had shown herself out there'd been no one to perform this service, so McCoy went to do it now.

When she got to the door a shiver ran through her: it was already locked. *She's still in the house! What the devil's she up to?*

McCoy carefully took off her nursing chatelaine so she could move about without a clacking bundle of tools announcing her position. She held the chains together to keep them quiet and softly laid the chatelaine on the marble-topped table next to the door.

She still believed Esmerelda was playing this game for all or nothing odds and wouldn't risk exposure by petty larceny. She wouldn't be after the silver or any of the small valuables on the first floor of the house; if she did manage to reel in Silas they'd be hers soon anyways, so there was no point in stealing them now. Whatever she was doing must be something she thought would strengthen her position with Silas, somehow. McCoy headed up to his bedroom, moving as quietly as possible. *Did she find out all those details by spying on him, and now she's looking for more information?* McCoy wondered.

Esmerelda wasn't in Silas' room. McCoy's next thought was that the woman was trying to interfere with her in some way and might be in her room, but she wasn't there either.

There was no reason for Esmerelda to be in any of the empty rooms. The only remaining inhabited chamber was Jacob's room on the third floor; he was currently off on his honeymoon but it still had all his personal things in it. McCoy rushed up there as fast as she could move while still keeping reasonably quiet.

Again, there was no one there.

Well, if this don't beat all! McCoy frowned to herself, looking at Jacob's desk, his bed and his washstand. *Was I wrong about that door still being locked?* She went to the window and peered out, looking for Esmerelda's retreating form on the road.

The sound of footsteps mounted the stairs to the third floor. *Aha!*

It suddenly occurred to McCoy that Esmerelda wouldn't have known *which* rooms were empty, so she must have been checking them all. *But why would she be looking for Jacob's room, after she already found Silas' and mine?*

McCoy rushed out the chamber door, determined to at least expose Esmerelda for a snoop. In her haste she forgot to tread stealthily, and the quick steps of her sturdy boots made the floorboards squeal.

There was a sudden flutter and flight of silk down the stairs. McCoy managed to get just a glimpse of one edge of Esmerelda's skirts as she disappeared around the corner into the groundfloor hallway. By the time McCoy reached the bottom of the stairs herself, the hallway was empty and the front door was unlocked.

McCoy rushed outside and saw Esmerelda standing by a currant bush affecting a look of innocence. "Such a lovely evening, don't you think?" She asked McCoy, grinning venomously. "I really couldn't resist stopping a moment in the garden here."

McCoy glared balefully at her, then a quiet hissing sound came from some nearby ferns. She looked over and saw the stray cat arching her back at Esmerelda.

"My sentiments exactly," McCoy told the cat.

Esmerelda laughed unconcernedly. She gave a haughty toss of her head, then pranced away without further discussion. McCoy scooped up the cat and carried her inside, intending to give her an extra-large piece of liver after she'd served Silas his supper.

I don't have any proof Esmerelda was snooping around, McCoy reflected in great irritation. *Would Mr. Hayes even believe me if I tried to tell him?* She frowned, absently scratching the cat behind the ears as she walked to the kitchen with her. *Hard to say. It would just be her word against mine.*

McCoy's last job had been taking care of an old woman whose niece's extravagant tastes exceeded her allowance of pin money. When some of the old woman's jewelry went missing, all the servants knew that the niece was to blame, but McCoy was the only one with the brass to say so. Instead of any thanks for speaking the God's-honest truth, she got sacked instead when the niece turned around and accused her of the theft. The old woman's health had been getting better anyway so McCoy didn't mind moving on, but still the whole business had left a bitter taste in her mouth and she didn't desire to re-live it.

McCoy had to expose Esmerelda —and soon. There was no question about that. But stories about locked doors and skirts glimpsed around corners weren't enough to do that, so McCoy decided to keep her own council for the time being.

Reaching the kitchen she set down the cat, washed her hands, and dished out Silas' dinner. While she'd been chasing Esmerelda the panada had burned slightly to the bottom of the pan so she took care not to scoop the scorched portions into his dish.

What was she looking for? McCoy mused as she poured the beef tea into a mug. *If she wanted something from Mr. Hayes' room or mine, she would have stopped at one of them. There wouldn't be any reason for her to continue up to the third floor except to look for Mr. Simmons' room —but what on earth could she want up there? She's never even met the man. He was off on his honeymoon already when she came.*

The cat miaowed hungrily, eyeing the beef tea. McCoy had made a little too much for the mug, so she poured the extra into a saucer and put it on the floor. The cat raced over and greedily started lapping up the broth.

McCoy chuckled, putting the mug and dish of panada on a tray. "Well, it wasn't intended for you, but I'm glad—"

She stopped suddenly. "It wasn't intended for you…" she repeated slowly.

She remembered how this whole shady business with Esmerelda had started with the arrival of a letter. A letter addressed not to Silas, but to his nephew.

She frowned.

Over supper McCoy asked when Mr. Simmons and his new wife were due back from their honeymoon.

"Early November," Silas answered. "After the hectic summer they had setting up the shop they certainly deserve some time to catch their breath again. Jacob said this is the slow season for his cycling business now, so there's no pressing need for them to hurry back."

Except that at the rate things are going, by the time they get home there could be an awful mess waiting for them, McCoy reflected.

She didn't like the idea of waiting three weeks for Mr. Simmons to come back and just counting on him having some light to shed on the matter of Esmerelda when he did. She supposed she could telegraph him, but what would she say? YOUR UNCLE MAKING A FOOL OF HIMSELF STOP HAVE YOU EVER KNOWN A WOMAN WHO NOW CALLS HERSELF ESMERELDA STOP

McCoy shook her head.

Silas noticed the action and asked if she was alright.

She sucked at the corner of her mouth. "I was wonderin': how much do we know about this Esmerelda character, really? You spent all afternoon with her; did she ever once say what she came out here for?"

"She said the spirits sent her."

McCoy cast her eyes upwards towards the ceiling.

Silas looked at her curiously. "Why are you so worried about her, McCoy?"

"Because all her talk about spirits is unadulterated humbug, that's why!"

McCoy almost thought Silas seemed pleased to see her so irritated. "I'd have thought you'd be happy to see me being civil to a guest," he suggested.

If McCoy hadn't known better, she'd have thought he was teasing her.

"I don't count a creature like that as a guest!" She snapped in irritation. "Can't you see she's just after your money?"

He winced.

McCoy folded her arms and sat waiting for an answer.

Silas looked down at his half-eaten panada, then set his spoon aside and gazed off towards the kitchen. "You know," he ventured after a while. "The first time I met Adora, I accused her of something like that."

McCoy perked up her ears. She'd never heard exactly *what* Silas had said to Addie before McCoy had found her hiding in a bunch of willow bushes crying her eyes out. "Go on."

"It was pretty obvious she was interested in Jacob—"

"Head over heels in love with him, you mean!" McCoy interrupted. "—Nearly as bad as he was for her! I could tell from the first time they clapped eyes on each other back at the dock."

Silas bowed his head shamefully, then slowly nodded. "I know that now, McCoy. But at the time... Well, I hadn't seen them together, and I hadn't seen the way he looks at her. I just thought—" He stopped and shook his head shamefacedly.

"What did you think?" McCoy prodded.

He picked up his spoon and poked at his panada, avoiding her gaze. "Jacob and his parents are the only family I have. I thought it should be pretty obvious to anyone that he'll be my heir. And I—" He stopped talking.

"—And you accused that poor, sweet Adora Kellam of being a fortune hunter," she concluded for him. "—Even though if you'd seen her face —like I did— back on the dock when she found out Jacob Simmons was your nephew, you'd have seen plain as day that she thought having a cantankerous old grouch like you in the family tree was a mark against your nephew, and in no way in his favor."

Silas continued poking at his panada, red-faced with shame. "I misjudged her," he agreed quietly. Then he looked up. "But, you see: you're accusing Miss Gracilis of the same thing. Don't you think you might be misjudging her, the way I misjudged Adora?"

"Esmerelda Gracilis is not Mrs. Simmons," McCoy told him flatly.

Something tickled at the back of her mind. What she'd just said seemed important, but she couldn't quite connect the edges together yet.

Silas broke in on McCoy's musings with a deep sigh. "I'm tired, McCoy." He rose slowly from his chair. "I'm going up to bed."

"It ain't even seven yet!"

He shrugged and continued upstairs.

Chapter XV

The next couple weeks followed much the same pattern, with Esmerelda and Silas spending long hours together and McCoy growing increasingly worried as they seemed to become more intimate. She occasionally wondered how Kitty was doing after her tearful exit from the seance, but she had more pressing concerns with keeping Silas out of trouble and she reckoned Dr. Brown could take care of his wife.

At first McCoy took solace in the fact that at least the cat seemed to distrust Esmerelda as much as she did. Every time Puss and Esmerelda crossed each other's paths, the animal would arch her back and hiss viciously. Then one morning this pattern changed suddenly. McCoy felt downright betrayed when the cat, seeing Esmerelda enter the parlor with Silas, ran in after them with a friendly attitude.

Dumbfounded, McCoy followed them into the parlor and watched, appalled, as the cat sniffed the air then ran up to Esmerelda and rubbed against her, purring happily.

Esmerelda smiled over at Silas. "Cats are so sympathetic, don't you think? They're such good judges of character."

McCoy watched the performance with mouth agape, then she remembered the very first time she'd seen this cat and an explanation occurred to her. She strode over, grabbed Esmerelda's hand and sniffed it, the way a suspicious dog would.

"McCoy, what are you doing?" Silas asked in alarm.

McCoy threw aside Esmerelda's hand as if it were a dead rodent. "Sniffin' a rat," she answered in disgust.

She grabbed the cat without a further word and marched out to the kitchen garden with her. She plopped the animal down in the middle of the catnip bush. "There's a bigger bag of silver for you, Judas!" She told the cat disgustedly. "I can smell when catnip's been rubbed on something, same as you. I just don't go losin' my head over the stuff!"

If McCoy had been a different sort of woman she'd have broken down crying, she was so frustrated. Instead, she went back to the woodshed and chopped kindling until her arms were sore.

When she finally stopped and looked around at the pile of splinters she'd created, she heaved a deep sigh. After a moment she heard something rustle behind her. She looked back and saw the cat.

"Miaow?" The cat looked at her curiously.

"Benedict Arnold!" McCoy hissed, glaring at the animal.

She remembered Silas' middle name: Benedick, from his Shakespeare-loving parents. *How had Esmerelda known? How did she know any of the things that she knew?* McCoy looked up at the house. *And why was she trying to get into Mr. Simmons' room? What was she looking for?*

As she stood looking at the house, McCoy suddenly heard a buglet call. *The cycling club must be riding somewhere nearby,* she reflected. *Or at least Felix Halloway is, and he's got at least one other man with him—probably Ken Kellam.* Felix was the club bugler, but there'd be no reason for him to bother with signals if he was riding alone.

The buglet sounded again, a different set of notes this time. McCoy thought back on the bored, knowing look Felix had worn during the seance, and wondered if he could explain any of what had been going on lately.

I don't like asking for help, but— McCoy frowned down at her hands, which were red and sore. It had been ages since she'd chopped this much wood at a go, and moreover she'd foolishly attacked the pile without gloves. *I reckon even a McCoy can use help sometimes. He may be a reporter, but the Simmonses trust him, and Ken Kellam trusts him, and those folks are all Mr. Hayes' family so I reckon it's alright.*

McCoy wiped the sweat from her forehead and went inside to change clothes. At the foot of the stairs she looked up and saw Esmerelda halfway between the second and third floors, heading upwards.

"What d'ye think you're doin'?" McCoy demanded bruskly.

Esmerelda was clearly startled by McCoy's unexpected appearance, but she recovered quickly. "Mr. Hayes wanted me to get a book from his room and read to him."

"His room ain't on the third floor, it's on the second." *And you already know that from the snooping you've done already. What are you really after?*

Esmerelda went back down to the second floor and walked into Silas' room without hesitation.

McCoy shook her head. *I suppose she figures I'm worth lying to, but not worth keeping up the pretences that would make the lies plausible. Otherwise she'd at least have pretended not to know which room on the second floor was his.*

McCoy felt mad enough to spit.

***

Dr. Brown came by a little later for his regular fortnightly visit on Silas and McCoy relished the opportunity to interrupt whatever was going on in the parlor. She rushed the doctor into the house and hastily slid open the parlor door without knocking.

Silas and Esmerelda were in the same chiromancy pose McCoy had seen before, and she was once more reading his palm. When the door opened he glanced at McCoy then pulled his hand guiltily away.

Dr. Brown consulted his watch in mild surprise. "Is this an inconvenient time this week? I always come—"

"Yes, of course," Silas agreed quickly. "I just forgot about our appointment." He glanced at McCoy, then turned towards Esmerelda. "Miss Gracilis, will I see you again tomorrow?"

"Of course." Her smile still reminded McCoy of a cat preparing to eat a mouse.

Silas made a creaky bow, then he stooped and kissed the back of Esmerelda's hand. McCoy felt her blood boil.

Dr. Brown looked curiously at Silas, then at McCoy, at Esmerelda, then back at Silas again.

"I'll show you out!" McCoy proclaimed, steering the other woman towards the door as forcefully as she dared. After she'd ejected her from the house she slammed the front door and made very sure it was locked.

When she went back into the parlor Silas and Dr. Brown seemed to be enjoying some sort of private joke. McCoy, who couldn't imagine what was so amusing, plopped down in a armchair in the corner and sat fuming. For once she didn't even get down her knitting.

Dr. Brown made the usual inquiries into Silas' health, then suggested to McCoy that some mint tea might be good for all of them. She was still seething as she stormed into the kitchen.

There was already a kettle of hot water on the stove; McCoy pushed it to the hottest portion of the rangetop so it would boil, then brought the tea things from the dining room into the kitchen. She was surprised to see Dr. Brown slip in behind her a moment later.

She frowned at him. "What—"

"I just wanted a brief word with you, McCoy." He shut the door quietly behind himself. "From the look on your face a few minutes ago I was afraid you might be headed towards an apoplectic fit if I didn't say something."

"What the devil are you talkin' about?"

"Nurse McCoy—" Dr. Brown smiled gently and shook his head. "Didn't you notice Mr. Hayes make sure you were watching him before he kissed that woman's hand back there?"

"What are you saying?"

He shrugged. "I'm just suggesting that performance might have not have been for her benefit. It might have been for yours."

McCoy angrily folded her arms. "My job's just to take care of him —no more, no less."

"Oh, I agree completely. I just thought I'd point out what's going on so you don't misdiagnose the case."

McCoy filled the teapot and cups with hot water to warm them, then emptied the pot. She put in some mint and refilled it again from the now-boiling kettle. "If he is playing a game —and I ain't agreein' with you!" McCoy glared at the doctor. "But if he is playing a game, it's a foolish one. That Esmerelda character is dangerous."

"She's definitely strange —and I'm sure Felix is probably right that her real interest in Mr. Hayes has more to do with his money than anything else. But actually *dangerous*?" He shook his head. "Give Mr. Hayes some credit, McCoy. I'm sure an old contracts lawyer can watch out for his own interests."

"He's too lonely for his own good."

Dr. Brown sighed and nodded. "I've always said that about him."

"And besides, what about the other people she's frettin'?"

Dr. Brown suddenly grew very solemn, knowing she referred to his wife. "Kitty's been very — changeable recently. Now, I know that I have to expect a certain degree of that in her condition, but I didn't quite appreciate how hard it would be to deal with in my own wife. When we first realized she was expecting, she was so happy it was like watching a sunbeam come to life. Since all this started happening though, sometimes she'll just suddenly sink into melancholy and stare at her first husband's picture for long stretches at a time. When I try to distract her or make an effort to cheer her up, she just looks at me as though there were something about me that makes her feel guilty." He heaved a deep sigh and shook his head.

"Ain't that more than reason enough to send this Esmerelda packing?"

He frowned. "Adam Butler died instantly when he broke his neck after the snake spooked his horse. The thing Kitty keeps telling me, over and over again, is that she wishes she'd had a chance to say goodbye. What if that's all this is, McCoy? This whole nonsense humbug of calling up spirits —if it gives Kitty the chance she wants to say goodbye to her first husband, shouldn't I let her have that? If it makes her happy again, does it even matter that it's not real?"

"It always matters whether something's real or not," McCoy answered firmly.

Dr. Brown pressed his lips together. "I wish I shared your conviction in the matter."

McCoy checked the tea. *Another minute or so*, she decided.

Dr. Brown told her, "Kitty wants to come to another seance."

"Another one? After what happened last time?"

"The more I try to talk her out of it, the more she keeps insisting. She's actually started accusing me of being jealous."

120

"Of her dead first husband? That's awful harsh, ain't it?"

Dr. Brown nodded grimly.

McCoy cast the hot water out of the cups and replaced them on the tea tray. "Well, I can see as how you'd want her to work this out of her system."

"I just want to take care of her, Nurse McCoy. I'm trying to work out the best way to do that."

McCoy nodded and sucked at the corner of her mouth. "You know, Dr. Brown, it strikes me that maybe the thing that bothers your missus more than anything is the strange not-knowing-ness about all this. If she could just know for sure, one way or the other, don't you think it might help?"

"Maybe. I hope so."

"Well, then—" McCoy took a deep breath. "Let's give her what she wants. Let's have Mr. Hayes ask Esmerelda to perform another seance. Only this time we'll be looking for where the screw is loose."

He nodded slowly. "Alright."

McCoy recalled her earlier reflection that Felix had seemed less surprised than the rest of them at the tricks performed during the last seance. She wondered again if the young man might have any insights into how Esmerelda was performing her shams. She asked Dr. Brown, "Could you ask Felix Halloway to drop by here sometime before the next seance? I want to ask him a few things about the last one."

Dr. Brown looked surprised, but told her, "Sure, I can ask Felix to come up here. I don't know that he saw any more than the rest of us, though.

After all, it was Ken —not Felix— who spotted the trick with the scarf."

"Ask them both to come up. The more heads on this problem, the better."

"Alright, then."

McCoy picked up the tea tray and they returned to the parlor together.

Chapter XVI

Friday evening while Silas and Esmerelda were in the parlor, McCoy saw Ken and Felix approaching the house and went outside to meet them.

For once Felix was walking alongside his wheel and pushing it, rather than racing atop it at breakneck speed. Ken was keeping pace with him, riding his own bike very slowly and occasionally riding backwards or stopping to show off little gymnastic feats so he wouldn't outdistance his friend.

They waved at Nurse McCoy and as she approached she could hear them talking.

Felix muttered, "I can't believe Mrs. Goldstein doesn't know where her husband keeps his tools."

Ken shrugged. "Why would she?" He reached back with one foot until he was standing on the little step at the back of his bike, then he kept pedaling with one leg. "Anyhow, she said he'll be home soon and she'll send him over to loan you the wrench you need."

Felix frowned grumpily and pulled on his handlebars. They wiggled slightly and even McCoy could see something was loose.

Ken gave a light laugh, then hopped back onto his seat. "If you're gonna get so out of sorts about it when something goes wrong, you should carry your own wrench with you, Spark."

"I don't want extra weight when I'm trying to beat my records. Why don't you carry a wrench?"

Ken stood up in his seat and shifted his weight so that his stabilizing wheel came off the ground and he was balancing on just his big driving wheel. "I'm not the one whose head's loose."

They reached McCoy and Ken hopped down from his bike. "'Evening, Nurse McCoy."

"Good evening." She peered quizzically at Felix's wheel. "Something wrong?"

"Just a loose head." He wiggled his handlebars again. "It just needs tightening."

"I'd bet there's a wrench in Mr. Simmons' room—"

Felix shook his head. "I don't want to go rummaging through Jacob's things when he's not here. I'll just wait for David to bring over a wrench."

They reached the house and Ken and Felix braced their bikes against each other in the yard. They did it very casually, as though they'd put their wheels in that position many times before —which they probably had. It struck McCoy as an interesting configuration: two bicycles standing upright, without need of any support besides each other.

Felix turned to McCoy. "So, Dr. Brown said you wanted to talk to us?"

"That's right." She glanced at the young men's cycling knickers. "But the two of you will catch your deaths of cold, dressed like that, if we stay out here talking. Come into the kitchen where it's warm."

At the word "kitchen" they both brightened, and Ken asked if there was any cornbread left.

"No, but I made a Sally Lunn this morning. Y'all are welcome to it."

The men exchanged eager grins and followed her into the kitchen.

They dug into the Sally Lunn with appetites that would have put field hands to shame, smearing it with liberal quantities of blackberry jam. McCoy outlined the situation with Esmerelda and Silas.

After hearing her concerns, Felix leaned back in his chair. "Well, we're happy to help you out in whatever way we can." He cast an amused glance towards the door to the rest of the house. "I'll be perfectly honest with you though: I'll never understand how some men can lose all good sense when a woman enters the picture."

McCoy eyed him wryly. "Since you're a man yourself you oughtta be careful about passing judgements like that. A few of my cousins said just about exactly the same thing then had their own words come back to haunt them later. But anyways, I thought you might be able to shed some light on how Esmerelda's setting up her shams."

"Some of them." Felix spooned out some jam onto his Sally Lunn then passed the pot to Ken. "Not everything. I can tell you—"

A knock sounded on the front door, interrupting him.

"That'll be David with the wrench," Ken suggested, then took one last enormous bite of his Sally Lunn before setting it down.

They went outside and after a few pleasantries were exchanged between the cyclists, David Goldstein handed Felix a small wrench.

Felix and Ken unhooked their bikes from each other and Felix squinted at a bolt on his. As he used the wrench to tighten it, he told McCoy, "The bit about picking the right names off those lists is easy, but I can't explain the rappings, or how she got plain water to catch those papers on fire."

David frowned. "What's this about?"

Felix looked over at him. "Just a phony spiritualist playing parlor tricks and making mischief." He explained how Esmerelda had dropped their lists of names into the basin of water, igniting them instantly.

"Did she drop a speck of something shiny in with them?" David asked casually.

Felix, Ken and McCoy all looked at each other in surprise.

"She might have," Felix answered. "It was pretty dark in the room —there weren't any lamps lit, and just a single candle."

David nodded. "And you said the reaction happened instantly?"

They all nodded their heads vigorously.

"Probably potassium, then. Sodium would have taken a few seconds."

McCoy squinted at him. "Sorry? Could you explain that a little clearer?"

David smiled through his bushy beard. "Chemical potassium ignites when it touches water. The reaction's pretty dramatic, and it only takes the tiniest bit of potassium to make some sizeable flames. Was the woman who did this the same one who stopped Mrs. Brown's watch and got her so worked up?"

"That's right!" McCoy answered excitedly, glad someone was finally giving her some answers.

"I've been thinking about that. A magnet will throw off a watch's balance wheel. If that woman had a powerful enough magnet hidden in her clothes somewhere, she could have stopped Kitty's watch by holding it close enough to the magnet for a while."

McCoy remembered how Esmerelda had pressed Kitty's watch to her heart while shamming a transmission from the spirit world. "She probably had it hidden in her corset..." McCoy muttered.

David nodded and looked curiously at Felix's wheel. "How's the bike, Felix?"

Felix tugged at his handlebars. "All fixed, thanks." He handed back the wrench.

"Any time!" David turned to leave.

McCoy stopped him. "You know, that woman's performing another seance tomorrow. If you—"

David chuckled. "Thanks, but I think Rachel and I will leave these newfangled religions to you folks. If you need help with anything that doesn't involve minor explosions or getting our watches broken, let us know."

He bade them a friendly goodbye and returned to his home next door.

Chapter XVII

McCoy turned to Felix. "You said you could explain the lists —how she picked out one dead person's name from a list of six people?"

He nodded and leaned his bike against Ken's wheel again. "It was all in the way she gave her instructions. She told us to think of a dead person's name, then she told us to *mix it in* with five other names. The word 'mix' makes people think of the middle of things, so already it's unlikely we'd put it first or last. Then remember how she kept talking incessantly?"

McCoy nodded.

"That makes it hard to come up with a list of things of the top of your head. After all, we went in expecting to speak with one dead person, not come up with the names of five living or fictitious ones, like she urged us. So, everyone was writing slowly because they had to think of five names —five names of people far off, because she kept repeating how important it was that she couldn't possibly know them. Then, when she suddenly told us to write quickly, that was the cue to write the dead person's name. It was the one name we'd already prepared, so it was the fastest one to think of when she pushed us. She gave us that cue right as we all got to the third line on our papers. Given the way she'd coached us through everything else, that was already the space where we were most likely to put the dead person's name anyway."

McCoy remembered that her dead grandmother's name had, indeed, been the third one on her paper. "Did it work with you?" She asked Felix curiously.

He grinned and shook his head. "Nah. I could tell what she was doing. I wrote my chosen name dead last. The one she called out was the one I'd written third, though. If I'd cried foul I'm sure she'd have had some ready excuse —contrary spirits present, or some such nonsense."

She nodded, then asked, "How is it you're so clever about this sort of thing?"

He shrugged. "One of the first investigative pieces I ever wrote was on the tricks some mentalists were using to bilk people out of their savings. Their methods weren't really that different."

They were interrupted when the front door opened and Esmerelda came out. She gave the trio a suspicious look, then smiled slyly. She ignored McCoy and addressed the two young men. "Mr. Hayes tells me you'll be back for another seance tomorrow, along with the doctor and his wife."

The two men glanced at each other, then at McCoy. She hadn't had a chance yet to tell them she'd asked Silas to be sure to include them again. She thought their insights could be valuable.

"I suppose so," answered Ken.

Esmerelda gave him an appraising look. "The spirits are not at all friendly towards unbelievers, you know. Those who interfere with visitors from the spirit world inevitably find themselves in very uncomfortable positions."

Felix stepped up beside his friend and looked down at Esmerelda. "Any spirit that tries to put Ken in an uncomfortable position would have to deal with me first —and I'd like to see them try."

Esmerelda tossed her head disdainfully and continued on without a further word.

When she was out of earshot Felix commented, "She's trouble, alright." He looked over at McCoy. "You said she's still angling to hook Silas?"

McCoy nodded grimly.

Ken frowned. "That would be hard on Addie. When Esmerelda was throwing herself at Silas before and fawning all over him I just thought it was funny —she looked so ridiculous and he seemed so confused by it he looked terrified. But later on when I told my ma about it she pointed out how bad it would be for Addie if anything actually comes of it."

McCoy nodded agreement.

Felix looked puzzled. "What do you mean?"

McCoy told him, "Mr. and Mrs. Simmons were planning on coming back here to live when their honeymoon's over."

"Of course they are." Felix still looked puzzled. "Jacob was living here already and there's plenty of room."

"And it's good for Mr. Hayes to have family here with him," put in McCoy.

"So what's the problem?" Felix leaned over to pull up his socks.

"For Mrs. Simmons?" McCoy folded her arms in front of her. "The problem is it ain't her husband's house."

Ken nodded, an uncharacteristically serious expression on his face. "Addie was worried about that."

"Any woman would be," McCoy asserted.

Felix straightened and frowned. "I don't follow."

Ken looked up at the beautiful new Queen Anne mansion in front of them. "Addie was worried about the fact that she and Jacob aren't going to have a place of their own. Big as this place is, fancy as it is, it's not *theirs*. It's Silas' house, and when all's said and done Jacob and Addie are just poor relations. The night before her wedding, Addie was telling our mother she would have preferred starting out her life with Jacob in a much smaller place that was their own instead of this mansion where they're here on Silas' sufferance."

"Except they ain't on sufferance," put in McCoy. "Mr. Hayes needs them here. You men have no idea how good those two have been for him."

Ken smiled and nodded.

"I still don't see why Esmerelda's machinations are particularly bad for Addie," Felix was still frowning.

"I'm getting there." Ken rubbed at a scuff-mark on his bike's wooden grip. "When Addie was talking to our mother about her worries, Ma pointed out that it's the woman in charge of a house that makes it a home —and since Silas isn't married, as Jacob's wife Addie would, by default, be the woman in charge of all this." He took in the mansion with a sweep of his hand.

"About time, too!" McCoy unfolded her arms and put her hands on her hips. "Place like this needs a woman to look after it. Even if it were my place to do that —which it ain't— I ain't the type to oversee somethin' like this."

Ken smirked at the firmness of her assertion.

Felix rubbed his chin. "So you're saying that Addie's looking forward to managing this household—" Ken and McCoy both nodded. "But if Silas were to marry Esmerelda—"

McCoy shuddered, letting her hands fall to her sides. "Then *she'd* be in charge —and that sweet Adora Simmons would wind up playing second fiddle to a polecat."

Ken looked worried. Addie was, after all, his only sister. "What does Silas see in that Esmerelda character, anyways?"

McCoy sucked at the corner of her mouth. "She knows an awful lot about him."

"Things folks in town might have told her?" Felix asked quickly.

"No, that's the strange thing. She knows things it seems like nobody should know."

"Could she have wormed them out of Silas himself using tricks like the one she used with the names on the lists?"

McCoy remembered how dumbfounded Silas had been when Esmerelda called him Silas Benedick, and other things the woman had surprised him with, like his mother's last words. She shook her head. "I don't think so."

Felix pulled his mouth to one side, then shrugged. "We'll see if we have any more answers after tomorrow."

McCoy frowned. "I was hoping we could put an end to this tomorrow. All of this is affecting Mr. Hayes in a way I really don't like."

"Investigations can take time," Felix told her sympathetically. "Sometimes far more than one wants them to. We'll get to the bottom of things, though."

Ken twisted his grips thoughtfully. "Jacob and Addie are coming back soon..."

Felix hooked an arm around his shoulders. "We'll get all this cleared up for them."

"I hope so." Ken still looked concerned.

"We will —don't worry." Felix chucked him under the chin. "Cheer up, Tanglefoot! Come on, we've still got some light. On the way home you can practice that crazy handstand coast again."

Ken brightened. "I keep telling you, I'm going to pull that off one of these days."

"Well, no time like the present." Felix unbraced his bicycle from Ken's and used his knuckles to rap out a rhythm on one side of his handlebars. McCoy thought it sounded like one of his bugle calls.

The rhythm seemed to mean something to Ken, because he smiled and hopped on his bike. "Have a good evening, Nurse McCoy. We'll be here as early as we can after work tomorrow."

Felix tipped his hat to her and mounted his own bike, then the two men rode off together.

If McCoy had known how soon they would return —and why— she would have warned them not to be so casual as they headed off into the dusk.

Chapter XVIII

McCoy had just served Silas his dinner when suddenly there was a loud and insistent knocking on the front door.

Silas started at the unexpected commotion, spilling his broth. McCoy jumped to her feet. "Who in the—"

"Nurse McCoy! We need your help!" From outside Felix's voice called out loudly.

She grabbed a small lamp and ran to the door. She unlocked and threw it open; Felix was on the other side, raising his hand to knock again.

"What's going on?" She asked quickly.

"It's Ken—" Felix stepped aside and at the edge of the lamplight McCoy saw that Ken's face was ashen. "He broke his arm!"

McCoy urged them both inside. Felix wanted to race off and get Dr. Brown immediately, but McCoy ordered him to wait while she made sure the arm was really broken. "The doctor needs to know what he'll be dealing with so he brings the right kit," she explained, rushing them into the parlor and lighting the largest lamp in there. She didn't bother replacing the lamp's round shade but hurried over to examine Ken.

Felix was at his friend's side; McCoy unclipped her vesta from her nursing chatelaine and slapped the box of matches into his hand. "Light the rest of the lamps!"

He rushed to obey, grateful for a way to actively help.

Ken's left arm was crooked and at strange angles, but his clothes made diagnosis impossible. "We'll have to get that sleeve off," McCoy told him, reaching for the scissors on her chatelaine. "From your jacket and shirt both."

Ken groaned. "My ma will never let me hear the end of this," he predicted, but submitted docilely to McCoy cutting the fabric along the seams.

Felix finished lighting the lamps then speedily returned to his friend's side and squeezed his right shoulder.

"How'd this happen?" McCoy asked, cutting quickly.

Ken winced. "I was practicing getting into position for that handstand coast —the one I was telling all of you about the other night."

"Standing up on your bike's seat with one foot and raising the other leg up in the air?"

"That's right. I got the balance wrong and tipped over sideways."

When she exposed the arm McCoy frowned at what she saw. She subjected Ken to a few tests then instructed Felix, "Tell Dr. Brown the arm's not broken —although that might almost have been better. His elbow's dislocated. Run on quick now and get the doctor."

Felix pressed his friend's uninjured right hand. "Don't worry, Tanglefoot. I'll break all my records getting down to the doc's!"

Ken smiled weakly. "You just want to be the one with bragging rights at the end of the day, Spark."

Felix pressed his friend's hand again, then raced out the door with lightning speed.

136

"Let's get you somewhere you can lie down," McCoy told Ken. "You okay to walk upstairs?"

He gave her a small, wry grin. "I walked here from down the hill. It's my arm, not my leg."

McCoy nodded approvingly. "Dumbed right. Come on."

The empty rooms needed airing so McCoy brought him into her own bedroom. She made him sit down on her bed then lit all the lamps and opened her nurse's bag. "I've got some laudanum I can give you now," she offered. "—Or the doctor will have morphine when he gets here."

Ken shook his head. "No, thanks. I don't want either."

"It's gonna hurt like the blazes when he sets that elbow," McCoy warned him.

"It hurts like blazes now," he told her with a humorless laugh. "I'll live." He looked towards the bed's single pillow. McCoy grabbed some more cushions so he could lean back, and he gave her a grateful look as she placed them behind him. "Thanks."

She mixed some powdered willow bark in water and made him drink it, then told him to try to rest while they waited for the doctor.

Silas had seen some of the examinations that had gone on in the parlor and then followed them upstairs, peeping in anxiously from the hallway. McCoy motioned him to sit but to keep out of the way.

Felix was known for being the cycling club's fastest rider; he made it back to his friend's side several minutes ahead of the doctor's arrival. He was drenched in sweat despite the cool temperature of the October evening so McCoy ordered him to go upstairs and borrow some dry clothes from Jacob's room.

He shook his head and sat down by Ken's side. "I'll be fine."

"You'll catch a chill, sitting around like that," McCoy told him. "No sense in making a bad situation worse by you getting sick on top of Mr. Kellam being hurt."

"All my cycling clothes are wool —I'll be fine." Felix insisted. He regarded his hurt friend with concern as tender as if he'd been a woman.

McCoy frowned. The doctor was going to have to put Ken through some very considerable pain to set his elbow back in place: the ulnar nerve was in the elbow, and setting it again would feel like the worst assault on his funny-bone the young man had ever experienced. Considering how much concern Felix was showing for his friend, McCoy didn't want him to witness the scene that was about to occur.

"It ain't worth the risk," McCoy told him, grabbing her towel off its hook by her washstand and shoving it in his hand. "I've seen men even stronger than you catch chills that put them in their graves because they wouldn't take care of themselves. Go wash all that sweat off and find some dry clothes you can borrow. You're almost as tall as Mr. Simmons and there should be something up in his room that'll fit well enough."

Felix left reluctantly, offering Ken a few more words of encouragement before he went.

When the doctor arrived McCoy sent Silas out of the room. Ken bore up admirably under the exceedingly painful process of having his elbow set, and when it was over Dr. Brown praised the young man's fortitude.

While the doctor was arranging Ken's arm in a sling McCoy opened the door to the hallway again and let Felix and Silas back in. Felix was wearing a rough shirt that was too big for him and pair of wool trousers which bagged slightly at his ankles, held up by braces he'd had to adjust. At a little over six feet tall Felix was by no means a short man, but he still wasn't quite as tall as Jacob and it was obvious he was wearing borrowed clothes. He had dressed in such a hurry he hadn't adjusted the braces equally and the clip on his left shoulder was noticeably higher than the one on his right, giving him an asymmetrical look.

"How are you holding up, Tanglefoot?" Felix asked, quickly crossing to Ken's side and gazing on him with tender concern.

Dr. Brown answered for him. "He'll be off his bike for six weeks—"

Ken groaned.

"—But there's no reason he shouldn't make a full recovery."

Felix pressed Ken's right hand. "It could have been worse, Tanglefoot."

"Six weeks without riding!" Ken moaned plaintively.

Felix patted his shoulder. "The rainy weather will start soon and the roads will be too muddy for good riding anyway. At least this didn't happen in June —you'd have lost the best season!"

Ken nodded glumly, clearly finding scant solace in this.

Felix turned to Silas. "Our bikes are out in your yard. Do you mind if I put them in your carriage house before I walk Ken home?"

Silas frowned. "I wouldn't think of letting you do that."

Everyone turned towards him with astonished looks. Seeing their surprise, he elaborated, "You're more than welcome to put your cycles in the carriage house, but I wouldn't think of making Ken walk home through the woods in the state he's in. It's at least three miles to his house, and it's dark already."

"You've got a point," Dr. Brown agreed. "The Goldsteins have a wagon and they're right next door. Felix, can you go ask David—"

Silas shook his head. "He should stay here through the weekend, at the very least, and as long after that as he wants to. There's plenty of room — and besides, I've already got a trained nurse here! A good one."

McCoy allowed herself a prideful smile.

"You'll stay, won't you Ken?" Silas asked. "We're family, after all."

Ken smiled, but hesitated. "I've got to work tomorrow—" he began.

Dr. Brown cut him off. "No, you don't! I'll take care of that. I'll drop by the shipping office first thing tomorrow and arrange for them to give you a few days off, doctor's orders."

"And I'll let your mother know where you are," Felix volunteered. He checked his watch. "She's probably worried. Dinner time at your house was half an hour ago, and if *you're* late for dinner, she'll definitely know something's wrong."

"That's all settled then," concluded Silas. "You're staying here. McCoy, would you mind setting him up in one of the spare rooms?"

It suddenly struck McCoy that this was a perfect opportunity to set Ken up as a guard dog in Jacob's room; his presence there would keep Esmerelda out of whatever mischief she kept trying to sneak upstairs to accomplish. "What about putting him in Mr. Simmons' room?" She suggested. "It's all nice and aired. Those spare rooms are so dusty. Dr. Brown, don't you think it would be more hygienic?"

Dr. Brown nodded. "Good thinking, Nurse McCoy." He looked at Ken. "You don't want to start sneezing or coughing and jostle that elbow. A clean room would be much better than one that's been empty a while gathering dust."

"That's that, then!" McCoy concluded authoritatively. "Let's get you settled upstairs."

Chapter XIX

When Ken discovered a stack of cycling-related trade journals in Jacob's room, he declared that he couldn't think of a better place to convalesce. His mother came by later in the evening with his nightshirt, toilet kit, a change of clothes, and (clearly knowing her son's prodigious appetite) an enormous apple pie. She interrogated McCoy a while on the state of the case, but left seeming satisfied that her son was in good hands.

The next morning Dr. Brown came to the house just as Ken and Silas were finishing breakfast in the dining room. He asked how Ken had passed the night, then let him know that he'd already arranged for him to have some time off from the shipping office. Ken thanked him, but told Dr. Brown he thought he might be cosseting him a bit too much. "I'm a clerk, not a wharf rat!" He told him with amusement. "It's not like I have to shift boxes of freight around. I just figure sums and do paperwork all day —and I'm right-handed! It was my *left* elbow I dislocated." He held up his uninjured writing hand and wiggled his fingers. "I honestly don't see what the issue is."

Dr. Brown smiled. "Just be grateful for the time off, Ken. You can afford to take a few days off: you live with your mother, so it's not like you have to worry about rent at the end of the month if you lose a few days' pay. I'm sure the shipping office won't collapse in your absence."

Ken shrugged, then winced when the action moved his sling. "You're the doc', Doc."

Dr. Brown looked around the table at McCoy and Silas. "Under the circumstances, don't you think we should cancel that seance that was supposed to happen tonight?"

Silas started to nod but before he could say anything Ken spoke up. "Don't go cancelling anything on my account. I'll be fine, really." He suddenly looked thoughtful, clearly remembering the last seance. "Doc, is Kitty…" He let the question trail off.

"Still angry about last time?" Dr. Brown finished for him.

Ken nodded sheepishly. "I think she's been avoiding me when I've tried to come by your house and apologize."

Dr. Brown folded his arms and gave Ken a stern look. "She has been. But after she heard about you getting hurt last night she was too worried about you to stay angry. When I left home this morning she was starting a batch of those coasting cookies you like so much, for a treat while you're recuperating." He sighed and shook his head. "She's very fond of you, Ken."

Ken hung his head.

McCoy eyed the doctor in irritation. "He didn't do anything wrong, you know. I just wish he'd caught that glowing silk and exposed the whole fraud. If he'd managed that, we'd be done with all this phony spiritualism by now."

An uncomfortable silence fell over the assembled group. Silas fidgeted nervously, then excused himself from the table and left the room. After he'd gone McCoy asked the doctor, "Isn't that the whole point of why we're letting that woman conduct another seance tonight? We're doing it so we can expose her, aren't we?"

Dr. Brown nodded, but retained his stern expression. "Yes, but it needs to be done tactfully." He looked from Ken to McCoy. "I fully understand that I'm probably wasting my breath with what I'm about to say —I might as well ask a man to fly to heaven on the tail of a kite as to expect either of you to exercise discretion. But we all need to use some judgment about how we reveal these things. For Kitty's sake—" He eyed Ken, who hung his head. "And for Silas'." He looked at McCoy.

Ken promised he would try, and McCoy reluctantly agreed. As Dr. Brown left, she couldn't help reflecting that Esmerelda was not restricted by any such oaths of tact or subtlety.

Chapter XX

By the time Esmerelda arrived that evening most of the group from the last seance had already been at Silas' house for hours. Felix came early in the morning, just after the doctor left. He brought his reporting notebook with him, and after checking that Ken was alright he spent the rest of the day working quietly in a corner, ready in case his friend might need anything. Ken and Silas spent the time playing chess, with Silas handicapping himself by progressively more pieces as he grew increasingly frustrated by Ken's lack of skill at the game. Mrs. Brown arrived early in the afternoon with a big bag of cookies in hand and tutted over Ken's injury more than his own mother had done. Meanwhile, McCoy knitted and thought anxiously about the evening to come.

If Esmerelda has us make lists again, I'll know the trick this time. She reflected. *Pay attention to how she's saying things, and don't put the answer she wants where she wants it.*

She felt for the pincushion on her chatelaine and made sure it was well-stocked. *If she tries to use a magnet to stop any watches again, that will be easy to show up as a sham. All I have to do is drop some pins on her. She'll look mighty silly with a handful of pins sticking flat-sides down on her bosom.*

When the evening grew dim McCoy moved around the parlor lighting the lamps. At first the homey smell of the kerosene and the extra illumination seemed to lift everyone's spirits. After the oil had warmed and the smell dissipated though, the bright glow inside the parlor seemed only to accentuate the dying of the light outside.

After what had happened at the last seance McCoy doubted that Esmerelda would try the trick with the luminescent silk again, and since she hadn't repeated the request for a basin of water she obviously wouldn't be using the potassium trick again either. As McCoy cast on the stitches in her knitting she wished she knew what the woman would try instead. *I'll just have to keep a sharp eye out for anything.*

Thinking about the basin of water made McCoy realize she was thirsty, and that others in the room probably were as well. She went into the dining room for some glasses and got a pitcher of water from the kitchen. The cat was scratching at the kitchen door so McCoy let her inside. The little animal followed her into the parlor and Kitty pulled her into her lap, seeming glad for the comfort the creature provided. After McCoy finished serving around the water a ringing of the doorbell signaled the doctor's arrival.

Dr. Brown had brought a lantern for later when he and his wife walked home from the seance. McCoy put it away in the kitchen for him then rejoined the group in the parlor. As the time of the seance approached eyes started glancing nervously towards the clock. A tense atmosphere began building in the room, like the feeling of the air before a thunderstorm. Kitty shivered; the doctor moved his chair close to hers and put an arm protectively around her. McCoy added an extra log to the parlor fire; it had been mostly fir before but now the spicy, pungent scent of burning cedar crept into the air.

Thick clouds masked the moonlight and the night outside was ominously dark. When Esmerelda appeared at the front door in the same long cloak she had worn for the last seance, her pale face stood out with a spectral air.

This ends tonight, McCoy told herself as Esmerelda strode past her into the parlor and both Silas and Kitty took on the same looks of fearful awe they had worn at the last seance. *I know deep-down they're sensible folks, though she's got them humbugged for now. I just need to show them how she's doing it, and we'll all be done with this nonsense.*

The cat in Kitty's lap eyed Esmerelda with intense interest. It wasn't the same catnip-induced glee the animal had shown before, but rather more like the interest she would have shown a dangerous and unpredictable rodent. The feline sat up and made quiet hunting chirps in the back of her throat. Kitty frowned in surprise, but she and McCoy were the only ones who noticed.

Silas met Esmerelda at the parlor door and she greeted him with the same unseemly familiarity she had shown previously. Silas seemed embarrassed at first, then he glanced quickly over at McCoy and finally stooped to kiss Esmerelda's hand.

That definitely ends tonight! McCoy vowed privately.

Esmerelda looked around the room. When she noticed Ken's arm in a sling her eyes went wide for a second and she swallowed. She shifted something underneath her long cloak and McCoy thought the woman almost seemed to be having second thoughts about something. However, Esmerelda soon defeated the twinge of guilt and regained control of her features. "I see my prophecy has come true," she told Ken with a pitying air. "I tried to warn you that the spirits are offended by disbelief. I'm sorry to see where your doubts have led you."

An angry look came into Felix's face that made McCoy reflect that Esmerelda was very lucky to be a woman. If a man had said such a thing, Felix would have knocked him down and mopped the floor with him.

Ken just laughed, though. "I fell off my bike trying to do a handstand on my seat. Spirits had nothing to do with it."

Esmerelda sighed. "I'm sorry to hear that you still don't believe." She shook her head sadly. Felix continued to eye her with angry suspicion, but Ken just smirked.

Esmerelda was still wearing her long cloak. McCoy stepped beside her and laid a hand on her shoulder. "Let me take that cloak for you—" McCoy tried to lift the cloak as she spoke the words, but Esmerelda was too quick for her. She clutched the edges of the cloak and quickly moved away. McCoy had to choose between ripping the cloak off her by sheer force or letting her go. Remembering Dr. Brown's plea for subtlety, McCoy let Esmerelda go —but not without a private curse for the lost opportunity. *Last time she had a music box and a phony silk ghost on a pole under there. What's she hiding this time?*

"I need some time alone before we start," Esmerelda declared. "Just a few minutes to commune with my spirit guide."

"Whatever you're gonna do, you can do it in full view of all of us!" McCoy told her emphatically.

"I should think so," Dr. Brown agreed. He stood, but made no move towards the door.

Esmerelda hesitated, then whispered something to Silas. He looked startled, then embarrassed. "Give her the room," he told the others.

"Mr. Hayes!" McCoy planted her feet. "That woman—"

"Just give her a few minutes, everyone." He looked nervously at Esmerelda.

Kitty rose and left the room, bringing the cat with her. Dr. Brown frowned, but followed his wife.

McCoy faced off against Esmerelda, ready to tear her cloak off and strip her skirts away too, if necessary. Then Ken passed between them.

"Remember what Dr. Brown told us," he whispered quietly.

McCoy huffed impatiently, but followed the others out of the room.

"Do you mind tellin' us what in the Sam-Hill that woman said to you?" McCoy demanded of Silas.

He fidgeted, looking profoundly uncomfortable. "Er... um..." He cleared his throat.

Dr. Brown asked, "What is it, Mr. Hayes?"

"She said..." Silas colored with embarrassment and avoided everyone's gaze. "She said that sometimes when she first calls up the spirits, certain spirits…" He cleared his throat again. "She said certain spirits… er, have an effect on her that wouldn't be seemly for other people to see."

"Oh, for land's sakes!" McCoy pointed an angry finger at Silas. "I appreciate your chivalry, but I'm gettin' a mite tired of your simplicity! Now, you—"

"Nurse McCoy!" Dr. Brown said sharply. "Control yourself!"

McCoy heaved a deep, angry breath, folded her arms, and stood there glaring at Silas and Dr. Brown until they all heard tinkling music emanating from the parlor.

Dr. Brown knocked on the door and Esmerelda called for them to enter.

She had banked the fire and turned out the lamps. The room was very dark, lit by only a single candle as it had been at the first seance. Esmerelda sat alone at the round table which had been brought in from the dining room. She'd unpinned her hair again and it flowed down her back, a shimmering brunette river.

The dining room chairs the rest of them had sat at around the table last time were pushed into corner behind some potted palms. It was clear they weren't meant to join Esmerelda around the table this time, but rather resume the seats they'd had on the usual parlor furniture when she arrived.

As at the first seance, Ken and Felix were the first to enter the room. They moved towards the seats they had just vacated, then Felix seemed to change his mind. He eyed Esmerelda distrustfully, then steered Ken towards the other side of the room.

Kitty sat in Ken's former place, it being closest to the banked fire. McCoy thought she saw Esmerelda frown slightly when Kitty took Ken's place, but it was impossible to be certain in the darkened room.

As everyone else took their seats the cat slipped back into the parlor with them. The animal paced back and forth in a state of agitation, making the same hunting noises she had produced earlier.

The wind outside had gained strength. It blew in forceful gusts that made the mansion's walls shiver and creak, strong though they were.

The music box wound down. Esmerelda closed her eyes and held her hands over the candle in front of her, clear for all to see. They did not move, but faint knocks sounded in the room.

"We are all thus assembled!" Esmerelda proclaimed in a dramatic voice.

Kitty fidgeted nervously.

The cat kept stalking, and chittering.

"The first spirit we call is that of Lily Hayes!" Esmerelda called out.

The wind gusted. Raps sounded. Esmerelda made a show of concentrating. "She says… She says she's disappointed that her only son has never married."

McCoy, Ken and Felix all exchanged frowning glances in the dim candlelight.

"Well, I—" Silas looked uncomfortable. "What would she have me do?"

"She wants you to find a woman who is sympathetic to you, and young—"

And brown-haired and deceitful. McCoy called out, "If you really are talking to the spirit of Lily Hayes, prove it!"

Esmerelda opened her eyes. "Her last words—"

"We know you know them," McCoy cut her off.

Dr. Brown asked Silas gently, "Can you think of anything else it would be hard for a stranger to learn?"

"I—" Silas hesitated, and looked towards Esmerelda. "She knows so much…"

"Family!" McCoy suddenly called out. "Did your mother have brothers and sisters?"

He seemed surprised. "Why, yes—"

McCoy waved him to silence, then she challenged Esmerelda, "Tell us their names! All Mrs. Hayes' brothers and sisters' names!"

Dr. Brown leaned forward intently. So did Silas.

Esmerelda shut her eyes tightly and held a hand to her forehead. "Oh!" She made a great show of being in pain. "The spirits—"

Kitty whispered to Dr. Brown, "Elijah, help her."

"No!" Esmerelda called out, then her body calmed. "The first spirit has departed," she declared sadly. "But another comes in her place."

The wind roared outside. The cat stalked the room.

"An unsettled spirit with unfinished business—" Esmerelda declared. Then her eyes went wide, as though she saw something evil approaching.

"No!" She cried out. "No, I must banish it!" She made a theatrical move with her right hand but her left went behind her back.

Out of the very periphery of her vision McCoy saw a quick movement as something dark dropped from the ceiling and into Kitty's lap. It looked like a thick rope.

Kitty jerked, startled. Her hands went to her lap automatically, then her eyes opened wide with terror as she suddenly identified the coiling shape writhing in her lap.

McCoy finally understood why the cat was so agitated.

The thick, ropy creature slithering over Kitty's lap was a live snake.

Kitty screamed.

Chapter XXI

Everything in the room exploded into a blur of activity, rendered even more frantic by Kitty's hysterical screams.

McCoy rushed to light a lamp. She didn't bother replacing the shade but let it cast its full glare upon the chaos in the room. Kitty leaped to her feet in an attempt to run somewhere, anywhere, and the snake was cast upon the floor. It writhed and slithered like reptilian quicksilver across the oriental carpet, Ken and the cat both launching into immediate pursuit. Dr. Brown put his arms around his wife and desperately tried to calm her, but her screams continued unabated.

Esmerelda looked towards Silas, who was utterly bewildered by the havoc underway. She seemed about to run to him, but McCoy dashed to the woman and pinned both her arms with movements she'd learned from years of wrestling her three brothers and two dozen cousins. "You're a bigger snake than that varmint on the floor!" She hissed.

Kitty was too terrified to recognize her own husband's efforts to calm her. She fought against him with fear-maddened strength, raining blows down on his face, chest and shoulders. "Kitty, please!" Dr. Brown pleaded. "You'll hurt yourself!" He called out, "Felix! Run and tell David to hitch up his wagon! I need to get Kitty home!"

Felix rushed out the door.

After the first instinctual dash the cat backed off, leaving Ken to catch the snake on his own. He darted after the lightning-swift serpent as it zigzagged back and forth across the floor. If he'd had the use of both hands he would have caught it, but he was handicapped by his injury and the snake slipped past him time and time again.

Esmerelda squirmed in McCoy's grip. "Don't even try it!" McCoy scoffed. "Ain't no man on earth can out-wrestle a McCoy!"

Kitty continued to scream until she had no more breath, then drew in air in great, heaving gasps and let it out in choking sobs. She continued to flail and strike out against her husband. A particularly forceful blow landed right on his jaw. He called out, "McCoy! I need your help!"

At that same instant, the snake sped under a marble-topped table right towards Brown and Kitty. Ken lunged towards it and struck his dislocated elbow against the table with such a loud *Bang!* that even McCoy winced.

Ken instantly screwed up his face, then slumped slowly to the ground clutching his elbow.

McCoy cursed and released Esmerelda then ran over to Ken.

His eyes were squeezed tightly shut and he was gasping in pain, but when McCoy knelt over him he insisted weakly, "I'm fine! Help Kitty!"

Kitty's hysterical cries, half-sobs, half-screams now, continued to fill the air and she kept struggling against her husband's efforts to calm her.

McCoy grabbed a glass of water from the floor by someone's chair and dashed its contents full in Kitty's face.

Kitty choked and spluttered. Dr. Brown cast a brief, angry glance at McCoy then devoted his full attention to his wife again. He patted her on the back and told her over and over again that she was going to be alright. As she cleared her airways her hysterics subsided and she settled into quiet sobbing.

McCoy crouched over Ken and worked as quickly as possible to make sure he hadn't dislocated his elbow again.

The cat had re-entered the fray with the snake and the two animals were facing off like gladiators in an arena. The snake coiled; the cat crouched down low. They both struck out —the snake hurling itself through the air with fangs gaping while the cat darted with claws outstretched. The cat struck the snake a glancing blow then darted out of reach of the vicious maw at the last instant. She whirled around again to face her opponent and the snake recoiled for another strike. The snake struck out again and the cat leapt back, then she rushed forward with redoubled force, closed against her enemy, and ended the conflict with decisive finality.

McCoy checked around the room for Esmerelda. As soon as McCoy had let her go, the woman had rushed over to Silas and was weeping crocodile tears upon his shoulder. McCoy cursed inwardly: this was exactly what she'd foreseen when chaos erupted, and why she'd tackled Esmerelda as soon as she lit the lamp. There was no help for it now, though. More pressing crises needed her attention.

Against Ken's will she stayed with him long enough to make sure the bones of his arm were still in place. He forced himself to his feet, though his face still bore an expression of intense agony, and pushed her back towards Kitty.

Kitty was still crying, but in a softer way now. Her shrieks had subsided and she was collapsed in her husband's arms, no longer fighting him.

Felix ran through the door, panting, "David's bringing the wagon."

Dr. Brown lifted up his wife. "It's going to be alright, Kitty," he promised, then quickly told McCoy to come with them.

The remains of the snake were still in the middle of the floor. Seeing that the Browns would have to walk past it McCoy rushed in front of them and kicked it away. It skidded over the floor and stopped at Esmerelda's feet. "Have to clean up that mess later," McCoy muttered.

David Goldstein had brought his wagon as close to Silas' door as he possibly could. Dr. Brown climbed up next to him, cradling Kitty in his arms, and McCoy scrambled into the back. They set off towards the Browns' house through the stormy night.

Chapter XXII

At the Browns' house the doctor gave Kitty a drachm of *viburnum prunifolium*. He told her it was just to help her sleep but McCoy knew its real purpose was to prevent miscarriage. After the shock Kitty had just gone through McCoy sympathized with the worried look on Dr. Brown's face. She could detect it easily, though she could also tell he was working very hard to hide it from his wife.

McCoy lit the fire in the Browns' bedroom and set a kettle over it. Dr. Brown sat on the bed where his wife lay, massaging her head and saying soothing things to her. She neither spoke nor met his gaze.

When McCoy stepped away from the fire Dr. Brown discretely signaled that he wanted to speak with her in the next room. He gently laid his wife's head on her pillow, then kissed her forehead. She still said nothing.

McCoy and Dr. Brown went into the hallway and he closed the door behind them. "Do I need to go back up there and set Ken's elbow again?"

McCoy shook her head. "He thwacked it mighty hard, but he didn't dislocate it again. I made sure of that."

Dr. Brown heaved a deep sigh of relief. "At least that's one thing that didn't go as badly as it could have tonight."

"I hope he's got the sense to take some willow-bark powder out of the bag in my room. I know he won't touch the laudanum."

"You should go back as soon as we're sure Kitty's out of danger."

"I'll fix a mustard plaster for between her shoulders as soon as the water in that kettle heats. It'll draw the blood away from her pelvis and help keep her womb from going into contractions."

Dr. Brown nodded. "I thought that might be why you put the kettle on." He took a deep breath and cast a guilt-ridden look towards the bedroom door. "I should never have let her sit in Ken's place. I'm sure Esmerelda intended that snake for him because of the way he upset her first seance. Oh, why did it have to be a snake?" He groaned, thinking of his wife's mortal terror of the creatures.

"They're lazy at this time of year because it's getting cold. I reckon it was easy to catch."

Dr. Brown pressed his forehead against a clenched fist. "Felix guessed that woman would try something, why didn't I? I shouldn't have let anyone sit there, or I should have sat there myself!"

"It's no use crying over spilt milk," McCoy told him, then issued one of Nurse O'Reilly's truisms: "You can't deal with what might have been, you can only deal with what is."

Dr. Brown nodded solemnly and took a deep breath before he went back into the bedroom. McCoy raided the kitchen for ground mustard, a stoneware plate, a flannel rag and a tin pail. Then she rejoined the others.

Kitty lay silent, her face turned towards the wall with a deeply troubled expression. Dr. Brown told her Nurse McCoy was going to put a mustard plaster on her back so she wouldn't catch a chill after their ride through the storm. Kitty nodded mechanically. She undressed and lay on her stomach, but said nothing. Dr. Brown tucked the blankets over her legs and hips with great tenderness. He was clearly agonized by her refusal to speak to him.

McCoy laid the flannel rag on the plate and poured a copious amount of water over both, letting it overflow into the pail. When the plate was warmed through she tipped the extra water into the pail, wrung out the rag, then laid it back on the warm plate and sprinkled it with mustard powder. "Give me a few minutes alone with her," she told Dr. Brown.

He cast an anguished look at his wife. "I'll just be right on the other side of the door, Kitty," he promised. He ran a hand over her hair, then left her with McCoy.

McCoy lifted the mustard plaster off the plate and carefully applied it to Kitty's back. "Why won't you talk to him?"

Kitty took a deep, sobbing breath. "I don't have the slightest clue what to say."

"He's your husband —you should have something to say to him."

Kitty half-raised herself on her elbows. "I've had two husbands, Nurse McCoy!"

"Lie down!" McCoy ordered. "You'll knock the plaster off."

Kitty obeyed, then went on, "Adam and I promised each other 'until death do we part.' He kept that vow, I didn't! What does that make me?"

"A sensible woman who moved on with her life after her first husband was dead and buried. No one could ever fault you for that."

"I fault myself."

McCoy wished she had a married woman handy to talk some sense into Kitty. Since there was, however, no matron available, she determined to do her best. *Deal with what **is***, she reminded herself sternly.

"Here's how I see it," she told Kitty in her usual blunt, matter-of-fact tone. "—You've had the care of two good men. Both of them promised before God and the law to give you everything they had or ever would have, and both of them carried through on that promise. If your first husband cared for you half as much as the doctor does, then I guarantee that wherever he is now he still feels the same way. The only difference is now you don't have to do his laundry."

McCoy realized she was rambling. She frowned and sat down on the bed. "Dr. Brown told me he doesn't mind you still being in love with your first husband. Now, if he doesn't mind —if your living, breathing husband doesn't mind— do you really think it would bother the other one to know you found someone to take care of you, since he can't do it anymore?"

Kitty sniffed into her pillow. After a long pause she answered, "I suppose not."

"So instead of you wasting so much energy and fretting yourself sick trying to speak to your dead husband, how about I open that door and let your living one back in?"

Kitty seemed thoroughly ashamed of herself. She nodded.

McCoy let Dr. Brown back into the room. He entered very much in the capacity of Kitty's husband rather than her doctor. They spent the next while engaged in conversation which McCoy, as a good nurse, judiciously closed her ears to.

When the mustard plaster on Kitty's back grew cold McCoy wiped it off and helped her sit up. Dr. Brown pulled the blankets up around her.

"How are you feeling?" McCoy asked. "Any cramps?"

Kitty seemed surprised by the question. When she realized the implication of what McCoy was asking her eyes widened and her hands reached protectively towards her abdomen. "No. Thank the good Lord."

McCoy nodded curt approval. "Then let me rub your feet a bit, then after that I should get going." She moved to the floor by Kitty's feet and went to work massaging them.

After a few minutes Kitty ventured, "Ken was right, you know. About the silk. I've worked with so much of it over the years I should have— But I wanted so badly to believe."

Dr Brown put his arms around her and she leaned into his shoulder. "It's alright, Kitty." He stroked her hair.

A little later Kitty asked, "Do you really think the rest of it was all trickery, too?"

McCoy reported all she had learned from Felix and from David Goldstein: the trick with the lists of names, the way potassium ignites when it touches water, and how a watch can be stopped by a magnet pressed against its balance wheel.

Kitty grew more solemn with each piece of information, but she nodded. When McCoy finished rubbing her feet she heaved a deep sigh and stretched out her legs. She sighed again, then bent her knees and let her feet fall heavily to the floor, toes first. When her big toes hit, they made a distinct thumping sound.

McCoy started. "Do that again!"

Kitty frowned. "What do you mean?"

"With your feet! Do that again!"

Kitty seemed a bit perplexed, but she complied. Again a thump sounded.

"So that's how she did it!" McCoy immediately began stripping off her own shoes and socks.

Dr. Brown and Kitty looked at her in slight alarm. "McCoy, what are you doing?"

"That's how she did the raps without using her hands!" McCoy hit the floor with her big toe. It sounded muffled against the carpet so she strode over to the edge of the room and tried again on the bare floorboards. This time the sound was closer to the noises Esmerelda had produced. "She must have brought in a board with the rest of her kit, and hidden it under the table when she set up the room!"

McCoy kept trying until she could produce a reasonable facsimile of the raps they had all heard during the seances. As the knocks sounded she felt triumphant.

Kitty looked sad, but accepting. "It really was all just a lot of elaborate tricks then, wasn't it?"

McCoy stopped rapping and nodded.

Kitty looked down, then raised her eyes towards her husband.

"You've still got me, Kitty," he said gently, and kissed her forehead. She relaxed against him.

McCoy slipped out of the house. As she picked her way through the storm-tossed night, the one remaining mystery still preyed on her mind: how did Esmerelda know so much about Silas?

Chapter XXIII

It was far too dark to read her watch and she had no idea what time it was when she climbed the final steep hill to Silas' house. All she knew was that she was dog-tired but couldn't go to bed before she'd checked on both her patients. "All these dumbed fools who can't take care of themselves…" She muttered as she dragged herself up the stairs.

Silas' door was closed. She hoped he was asleep but even if he wasn't, a dislocated elbow took priority over fretful insomnia. She brought her nurse's bag from her room and headed upstairs to check on Ken.

The door to Jacob's room was ajar and —to McCoy's surprise— the door to the small room adjoining it was wide open. It was one of many empty rooms in the house and McCoy had never given it much thought beyond a mild speculation that Addie might use it as a sewing room when she moved in with Jacob. Seeing the door open was enough of a surprise to draw her attention; she glanced inside and detected the vague outline of a masculine form sprawled on the bed in there.

It occurred to her that Felix must have stayed to look after his friend. This suspicion was confirmed when, awakened by her tread outside his door, he rose and met McCoy in the hallway. He was still dressed, though his shoes were off. "Ken's asleep," he whispered, guessing why she'd come.

"No, I'm not!" Ken called out. "My wretched elbow hurts too much to sleep. I was trying to let you rest."

McCoy and Felix looked at each other, then they both joined Ken in Jacob's room.

McCoy lit a brass lamp with a green shade. The light fell on the glass-fronted bookshelf above Jacob's desk and lit up the long row of books lined up there.

There was only one chair; Felix left it for McCoy and sat down on the foot of the bed. "How are you doing, Tanglefoot?"

Ken sat up awkwardly. "I've had far better days but I'll live. Nurse McCoy, how's Kitty?"

"She'll be alright. She won't be attending any more seances, I'm sure of that." McCoy checked on Ken's elbow, dosed him with willow bark powder, then sat down on the chair. "What happened after I left with the Browns?"

Ken looked slightly sheepish. "I was mostly preoccupied with my elbow," he admitted.

"Ain't no shame in that," McCoy assured him. "You banged it mighty hard. Dr. Brown and I were both surprised you didn't dislocate it again."

Ken nodded and McCoy turned to Felix. He told her, "I spent the first few minutes working out what was wrong with Ken—"

That's right, McCoy remembered. *Halloway was already running for Mr. Goldstein when Kellam hit his elbow. He missed that whole scene.*

"—Then," he continued. "I saw that the snake was dead and that the cat was looking smug about it. Esmerelda was blubbering all over Mr. Hayes about how you'd hurt her—"

McCoy cast a scornful gaze skywards. "If I'd tried to hurt that mewling, milk-fed creature she

166

wouldn't have been in any position to moan about it afterwards, especially not standin' on two feet and wailing about it. Go on."

"Don't worry, I don't think Mr. Hayes believed her —and he was clearly very unhappy about the way things had gone. He ordered her to leave. She pled that the storm made it cruel to send her away, but since all of you had just fled out into it that excuse fell pretty flat. Then she went as far as a naturally shrewd and naturally lewd woman dare go (which was pretty far) to convince him to let her spend the night here. That just made him even more adamant that she needed to leave."

"Well, that's to the man's credit," McCoy said approvingly. "But I reckon we haven't seen the last of Esmerelda."

Felix nodded grim agreement.

McCoy stifled a yawn of exhaustion. She looked across the room and her eyes fell on the row of books with blank spines. She frowned at the way her attention kept being drawn to them.

"We know how that woman's done all her fool parlor tricks," McCoy mused. "But the thing we still don't know is how she knows so much about Mr. Hayes."

"Does she really know so very much about him?" Asked Felix.

"Too dumbed much." McCoy cited some of the strangely specific details that Silas had reported Esmerelda knowing.

Felix folded his arms and leaned back in his chair. "Sounds to me like she's been interviewing someone closely acquainted with him."

"Who?" McCoy asked. "His nephew was gone before that woman came to town, and Dr. Brown's pretty much his only friend. I know he didn't tell her those things."

"One of his old nurses, maybe?" Suggested Ken. "From what I've heard there have been enough of them who've come and gone over the years to staff a small hospital, and none of them left him on friendly terms."

McCoy sucked at the corner of her mouth. "He can be an ornery cuss to someone who doesn't know how to handle him, that's certain. But someone in service who a man throws bowls of porridge at is not the sort of person that same man confides his mother's last words to. No, it would have to be someone closer to him."

"Are you thinking of his family in New York —Jacob's mother and father?" Asked Felix.

McCoy thought of the New York postmark on the letter that started all the trouble. "Maybe." She sucked at the corner of her mouth again speculatively. "Those sort of details aren't the sort of thing someone says the first time they meet someone, though. She'd have to know them pretty well —and been taking notes on them."

"Why would anyone take notes on Jacob's folks?" Asked Ken. "As I understand it, they're poor as church mice."

"Silas isn't," Felix pointed out.

Ken ran his right hand through his hair tiredly. "This is getting too convoluted for me!"

Again, McCoy's eyes were drawn to the bookshelf atop Jacob's desk. "If she knew them for a while…" She stood and walked over to the glass-fronted shelves.

The key had been left carelessly in the lock. McCoy remembered Silas lecturing Jacob about his longtime habit of keeping his desk unlocked.

Felix eyed McCoy as she approached the desk. "What are you thinking, Nurse McCoy?"

She answered slowly, "I'm thinking that if Esmerelda knew the family in New York long enough to learn what she knows, maybe there's some sort of record of it." She peered at the tops of the blank-spined books and saw that the loose papers tucked into them were letters. She'd suspected as much.

Opening the glass door of that bookcase went against all her convictions that the privacy of the people she cared for was absolutely sacred. Keeping them safe and out of trouble was an even more basic duty though, and she forced herself to open the case. She took a book from the far right of the row of blank-spined volumes and handed it to Ken. "Check for me: that's a diary, isn't it?"

He seemed somewhat taken aback. "If it is, it's none of my business to be reading Jacob's diary."

"Nor mine, either. But you're more his family than I am. If there is mention of Esmerelda in there it would help us to know about it."

"I strongly doubt that's her real name," Felix commented. "If Jacob did meet her at some point it's anyone's guess what name she was using at the time. That's assuming he recorded the encounter at all."

"I admit it's long odds," McCoy agreed. "And you're right —if that's her real name then I'm the Queen of Sheba. But could be there's a description of her in there somewhere —and if there is, maybe the circumstances around it could tell us more about her."

Felix shook his head doubtfully. "That's a pretty wild stretch, Nurse McCoy."

"It's worth a try."

Ken very reluctantly took the book from McCoy and peeped inside its cover. "It is a diary," he confirmed. "Are you sure you really want me to read it?"

"If it'll help expose that fraudster," McCoy told him.

Felix walked over to the bookcase and regarded the long row of diaries on the shelf. "Based on the sheer number of these, I'd say they go back years and years —probably to when Jacob was a teenager. And you're looking for a vague reference to a description of someone he *might* have met once?" He shook his head and blew out his breath. "Talk about a needle in a haystack."

Ken asked McCoy dubiously, "Are you suggesting I read all that whole shelf of Jacob's private thoughts?" He frowned. "Why don't we just wait and *ask* Jacob if he knows Esmerelda? He and Addie will be home next week."

McCoy eyed Ken sideways. "Do you really want your sister plunked down into a scene like the one we just went through a few hours ago? Esmerelda would eat her alive."

Ken raised his eyebrows, then he frowned even more deeply. He obviously found the thought sobering.

"—And besides," McCoy went on. "Who knows what that woman will do in the meantime? Look at all the trouble she's caused already!"

"We could telegraph Jacob," Felix suggested. "Before he and Addie leave New York."

Ken bit his thumb thoughtfully. He was clearly imagining his sensitive sister in the middle of the chaos they'd all just witnessed. "Let's see if we can manage to leave Addie and Jacob out of this." He opened the book and started reading.

"If we're lucky maybe you won't have to go through more than one or two before you find something," McCoy commented. "If we're lucky." She folded her arms and regarded Felix a moment. "You told me once you don't give out your friends' secrets. Is that really true?"

"Yes, ma'am!" He assured her without hesitation.

McCoy squared her jaw and nodded. "You help him, then." She took down a diary from the other end of the shelf and handed it to Felix. "It'll go twice as fast with two people as with one."

Felix took the diary and nodded. "And you?"

McCoy picked up her nursing bag. "I'm going to check on Mr. Hayes." She stifled a yawn and blinked hard. She was so tired her eyes didn't want to focus. "Then I'm going to get some sleep before I fall over. Good luck!"

Chapter XXIV

Exhausted though she was when she retired, McCoy was still the first to stir the next morning. The night before she'd listened at the ventilation grate just long enough to decide Silas was already asleep, then fell into her own bed wearier than she'd been since her old days as a ward nurse.

When she woke in the morning she listened again at the grate long enough to confirm that Silas was still asleep, then she climbed up to the third floor to see if Ken and Felix might have turned up any useful information through reading Jacob's diaries.

Loud snores came from both rooms. Ken was tucked in more snugly than most people usually manage with two good arms, while Felix was sprawled on top of the bed in the next room, asleep in his clothes. From the look of things McCoy guessed Felix had forced himself to remain conscious as long as his friend's painful elbow had kept him awake. As soon as Ken fell asleep Felix carefully tucked him in, then collapsed on the bed in the next room, too tired to undress or even climb under the covers. McCoy approved of his diligent watch of the patient, but frowned when she saw the awkward angle of Felix's head on the bed. *If he sleeps much longer like that, he won't be able to turn his head for a day, at least. All these blamed fools...*

McCoy used some nursing tricks to move Felix under the bedclothes without waking him and positioned his head so he wouldn't wake up with a stiff neck. Then she went quietly back downstairs, leaving both men to rest.

It took longer than usual to get the kitchen stove going because she hadn't had a chance to lay a fresh fire the night before. After she'd done so she lit it and put the coffee on, slid the kettle to the middle of the range, then left things to heat while she went into the parlor to clean up last night's mess.

The cat had evidently carried off the snake's remains sometime in the night: the carcass was gone but a smear of blood remained on the carpet which no human would have left behind. *Should have thought of that.* McCoy got a scrub brush and bucket from the kitchen.

After returning to the parlor and opening the curtains she suddenly paused. *Halloway said Mr. Hayes sent Esmerelda away at short notice,* she recalled. *And presumably they didn't leave her alone in here before she went, so…*

McCoy looked up at the ceiling: there, on the broad expanse of ornately painted plaster she saw something that sent a thrill of triumph through her. *She didn't have time to take it down! She didn't have a chance to take it away with her!* McCoy felt like crowing. *If that doesn't convince him to give her the boot, I don't know what will!*

McCoy ran upstairs to Silas' room and burst in on him. "Wake up!" She ordered. "I need to show you something!"

A few minutes later they were both in the parlor, McCoy pointing at the chair where Kitty had been sitting the previous night. "That's where Mrs. Brown was, and if you look up—" She pointed in a straight line from the chair to the ceiling. A cloth bag was tacked up there, hanging open. "Still think that

Esmerelda was conjuring up spirits from beyond the grave?"

Silas grimly regarded the bag.

McCoy went on. "She tucked away the string she used to close the bag —I'm sure it had just been slip-knotted on, that's how she opened it so easily. If it was a black string we couldn't have seen it in the dark. It would have been easy to slip something like that in her pocket, especially with everyone distracted by Mrs. Brown's hysterics and the snake. I bet she even had time—" McCoy checked under the table: there was only carpet. "Yeah, she had time for that."

"For what?" Silas dropped his gaze from the ceiling to look at McCoy.

"To get rid of her plank."

"Her plank?"

For response McCoy took off her right shoe and sock then went over to the edge of the room. She peeled up an edge of the plush carpet and used her toes to rap loudly on the wood.

Silas watched her intently, understanding dawning. "She dropped her cloak on the floor when she took it off the table. You were gone already by that point. Then she picked up the cloak but didn't put it on. She just carried it in a bundle when she went out. It surprised me, considering how scantily she was dressed and how much she'd protested about the storm." He sat down heavily and ran a weary hand over his face. "If she was striking her toes against a board, like you just showed me, she must have hidden it under the cloak when she picked it up."

McCoy sat down in the chair next to him and put her sock and shoe back on. Then she looked pointedly up at the bag on the ceiling. "Do you really want the sort of woman who'd do that to Mrs. Brown prowling around here?"

Silas looked at McCoy, for once meeting her direct gaze with one of his own. "Of course not. I told her last night that after what had happened I didn't want her to come back here."

"And will you stand by that if she comes back anyway?"

"I will." He set his jaw, frowned, and looked away. "It's just strange that she knew so much, Het—" He stopped himself and amended, "McCoy."

McCoy nodded curtly.

A sad look came into Silas' face and he went on. "The things she told me— Well, maybe I'd known them all at some point in my life, but a lot of it was things I'd forgotten myself until she reminded me. She had to be getting all that information from somewhere. If everything she claimed about talking with spirits really was just lies and trickery, how did she know so much?"

McCoy frowned: she had no answer for him.

She heard footsteps outside the open parlor door and looked over her shoulder. Felix was standing in the hallway.

His clothes were wrinkled from sleeping in them but his hair was neatly combed. "Thanks for letting me spend the night to look after Ken," he told Silas. "Is there any breakfast I can bring up to him?"

"Coffee's probably close to ready," McCoy told him, rising. "Won't take but a minute or two to fix some eggs." She looked a question at Silas.

"An egg will be fine," he told her. "With some mint tea."

Felix followed McCoy into the kitchen. She moved the kettle to the hottest part of the range and put a large skillet near it. "Did the two of you find out anything last night?"

He shook his head. "Not much, I'm afraid." He glanced around the kitchen. "Dishes out in the china hutch?"

She nodded.

"I'll get them." He left the room.

The kettle started boiling as Felix came back into the kitchen. McCoy fixed Silas' tea and set up a soft-boiled egg for him, then she put some butter into the skillet and cracked a bowlful of eggs into it. "Stir these for me," she ordered Felix. "I'm sure even a man can manage *that*."

She brought the tea and soft-boiled egg out into the dining room, called Silas in to breakfast, then rejoined Felix. She eyed his work with the eggs suspiciously. "Not bad, for a man," she conceded. "Either of you take cream in your coffee?"

"None in mine, but Ken will take as much cream as you'll give him and up-end the sugar pot, too."

"Fair enough." McCoy got out the tray Silas' old nurses had used to bring him breakfast in bed and loaded it with the dishes, coffee, cream and sugar. "Those eggs done yet?"

"They're close. I don't suppose you've got any pepper sauce, do you?"

McCoy got her bottle of Tabasco sauce from the kitchen queen and added it to the tray. Then she peered at the eggs. "They'll be cooked by the time we get them upstairs. You carry them, I'll take the tray."

"You want me to carry them up still in the skillet?"

"Best way to keep them warm. Just make sure to bring a towel to put the pan on."

As they passed through the dining room McCoy put a plate on the table for herself and told Silas she'd be back down after she'd helped Felix carry things upstairs.

"Is Ken that much worse?" Silas asked, concerned. "He had his meals down here yesterday."

"He's just tired," Felix answered. "He didn't sleep much last night. The coffee should wake him up. I'll make sure he comes down after breakfast."

As soon as she was upstairs with both the men McCoy asked again how their search through Jacob's diaries had gone.

"You know, Nurse McCoy," Ken responded, putting more sugar in his cup than McCoy had seen anyone outside the South take with their coffee. "I would really appreciate it if you don't tell Jacob we did that. I had no idea any man could ever write such nauseatingly mawkish poetry about my sister." He made a disgusted face.

"Don't worry, I won't tell him. But what did you find?"

Felix divided the eggs, leaving some in the pan for McCoy. "There's entirely too much material in those diaries for two people to go through all of them in a week, let alone a single night. After a few hours we decided we had to narrow things down if we were ever going to get anywhere."

He drowned his eggs in Tabasco sauce. McCoy hoped he knew what he was doing.

He continued, "Since everything Esmerelda knows seems to be from around the time that Silas' parents passed away, we tried to look for the diary that covered that time frame." He took a large bite of his Tabasco-drenched eggs. His eyes widened, then he grinned. He picked up the bottle and gave the label an approving look.

"And?" McCoy prodded him.

Ken spoke up: "I thought I remembered something having come up in conversation once about Jacob's grandparents having died when he was eighteen. He dates all his diaries on the front endpapers, so we looked for one from '76."

McCoy looked at him eagerly. "And?" She repeated.

"Well, that's the strange thing. That one was missing."

Felix took over the explanation: "For every other year Jacob seems to have been one of the most diligent diarists I've ever known. He made entries practically every day since he learned to shave. But between early Spring of '76 and late Autumn of '77, there's a big gap where he didn't make any entries at all. At least none in these books."

"You're sure?" McCoy asked, excitement building as an idea started to form.

"We checked through all of them three times," Ken told her. "At first we thought it might just be out of order. Then we wondered if we'd just missed it because we were tired. But it's definitely not here."

"Some people fall in and out of diary writing," Felix offered. "It takes a lot of effort. Sometimes people just let it lapse for a while."

"But you said otherwise he was real regular?"

"There were the usual stops and starts when he first began and was still getting the hang of things," Felix told her. "But otherwise, yes. There's a couple very diligent years, then the gap, then back to entries as regular as ever. I'm actually really surprised he didn't bring his current one with him on his honeymoon."

"Addie gave him a special one for the trip," Ken explained. "Made it herself —spent a whole day on it. You know how sentimental she is."

Felix nodded agreement.

Ken went on, "Actually, considering how sentimental Jacob is too, I did have one thought about what might have happened to the missing diary — assuming there is one and he didn't just let it lapse." He paused, looking slightly reluctant to continue.

"What do you think happened to it?" Urged McCoy.

"Well, it's kind of morbid..." Ken rubbed the back of his neck. "But what if he buried it with his grandparents?"

"He's not Rossetti, Ken!" Felix scoffed. "And remember even he had second thoughts about the matter. Besides, burying a diary with his grandparents? If we were talking about some sweetheart of Jacob's I'd admit the possibility, but who buries a diary with his *grandparents*?"

Ken looked down at his eggs. "It was just a thought."

McCoy's idea was building. She asked excitedly, "Did you read the next diary?"

"The start of it." Felix scooped up more of his Tabasco-drenched eggs.

"Did it say anything about why the last one was missing?"

Felix shook his head, chewing.

Ken answered, "The first entry of the diary after the gap just says something along the lines of, 'The less said about the past few months, the better.'"

"Was that all?"

"There was a really vague reference to someone he regretted ever meeting."

McCoy's theory suddenly blossomed into a conviction. "Do either of you know where Esmerelda's been staying in town?"

The men seemed surprised by this apparent non-sequitur. They shook their heads.

McCoy hurried to the door. Seeing her sudden departure, Ken called out, "McCoy!"

She half-turned.

"Are you gonna eat those eggs?"

"They're all yours!" She rushed downstairs.

Chapter XXV

Silas didn't know where Esmerelda had been staying, either. McCoy didn't waste time berating him for having spent so many long hours with the woman and not learning such a basic thing about her; she simply grabbed her hat and shoulder wrap and hurried downtown as fast as she could go.

She took the steep shortcut through the woods, where the interwoven branches of cedars and firs turned cloudy mid-day to a dull twilight and the hoarse, barking voices of squirrels protested her invasion of their territories.

Downtown she asked at each of the city's hotels for a woman matching Esmerelda's description. She got the managers' full attention in each case by telling them Esmerelda was a diphtheria patient who had slipped off the quarantine island and by now would be in a highly contagious stage of the disease. The hotel keepers were eager to help when they heard this story, but none had rented a room to the woman McCoy described.

By the time she entered The Bishop hotel McCoy was starting to lose hope of catching Esmerelda at her lodgings. This was the last respectable hotel in town she hadn't tried yet, and she doubted she'd find Esmerelda in the other sort. Not that McCoy didn't feel Esmerelda belonged in the other sort; she simply believed the more regular woman lodgers in those places wouldn't tolerate out-of-town competition.

The Bishop's lounge was on the ground floor but all the rooms and the office were upstairs. The staircase had its own door; it was separate from the lounge and opened right onto the street. As McCoy climbed up the stairs to the office she noticed that the pressed plaster wainscotting on either side of the steps featured stylized pomegranates. Addie had once told her some old pagan yarn about the pomegranate being the symbol of the Queen of the Dead; seeing the plaster pomegranates on the wainscotting gave her hope that Esmerelda might be here after all. McCoy didn't set any store by superstition herself, but she figured a body didn't go in for Esmerelda's particular flavor of charlatanism without some degree of superstition. She judged that Esmerelda would have considered those symbols of the Queen of the Dead to be a good sign for someone in her line of work, and might have chosen this hotel because of them.

She reached the second floor and walked down the hall to the office. The door was closed and the man in the little room peered at her through a brass grill. He seemed politely curious.

"I'm looking for a patient who snuck out of quarantine a few weeks ago," she began, launching into the same story she'd been telling at different hotels throughout town.

The man behind the grill stepped back. McCoy had his full attention but he was clearly glad there was a barrier between them.

She continued, "She'll be a very dangerous woman to be around by now."

The man started sweating into his starched white collar. "What does she look like?"

"Taller than me—" McCoy held up her hand at Esmerelda's height. "Light brown hair, brown eyes, pale skin, comely in a sickly sort of way. Likes to drench herself in patchouly."

At the mention of patchouly the man went pale. "She's here!"

McCoy stepped up eagerly to the brass grate. "Which room?"

"Number thirteen."

"You got an extra key?"

He took a key off a hook from the wall behind him and held it out to McCoy at arm's-length through the grate.

She grabbed it from him and he pointed down the hall. "It's just over there," he told her nervously. "You passed it on your way in."

Room thirteen was in a corner by the stairs; it took McCoy just a few strides to reach it. She thrust the key in the lock, flung the door open, and—

Found the room deserted.

There were ammonia-like white stains on the carpet, likely from the turpentine Esmerelda had used in creating her luminous powder. An empty laudanum bottle lay on the floor and a wet cloth from the wash basin had been thoughtlessly tossed onto a wooden desk, where it was ruining the varnish. Judging from the smell of the room, a bottle of patchouly had been spilled somewhere. But Esmerelda was not there. Nor, tellingly, was any luggage.

McCoy turned to the office clerk, who had followed her at a cautious distance. "She pay up her bill?"

He looked in the room and saw the same lack of luggage McCoy had noticed. "No!" He responded angrily. "And from the look of things she won't, either! Of all the—"

McCoy plugged her nose at the patchouly. "I'd give this place a good scrubbing, if I were you."

He seemed to suddenly remember her tale of an escaped quarantine patient. "What would you recommend?"

"Lye soap and hot water —and plenty of both!" Without further conversation McCoy left the hotel and headed back towards Silas' house.

Chapter XXVI

Halfway up the trail through the woods, McCoy encountered Ken and Felix.

"Going home already?" She asked, surprised. "Mr. Hayes said you could stay as long as you like, and Dr. Brown got you that extra time off work."

Felix had been carrying Ken's grip for him; he set it down and they exchanged embarrassed looks.

Ken scuffed at the brown fir needles which carpeted the path. "To be perfectly honest, I'm not entirely comfortable staying in Jacob's room after reading his diaries."

"Pshaw!" McCoy shook her head at him. "You did him a service. I'm surprised you haven't worked that out yet." She continued up the hill.

As she stepped over a large root Ken called, "What do you mean?"

"Ain't got time to explain it now. I've got to get up to Mr. Hayes' place before Esmerelda does."

"But she's already been there," Felix told her. "Right after you left. She must have come up by the road while you were taking this route downtown." He indicated the steep footpath they were on. It was well-known to locals but unfamiliar to visitors.

McCoy's temper rose. "And you men left him alone with that woman?"

"No, he sent her away." Ken adjusted his sling. "He was practically shaking in his shoes when he did it. I couldn't tell whether it was more because he was afraid of Esmerelda or because he was so angry about what she'd done to Kitty."

"I think it was about equal parts," Felix put in. "He wouldn't even let her in the house. He just told her that her presence was no longer welcome and sent her away. I wanted to make sure she wouldn't try any last-minute mischief so I ran upstairs and watched from the windows in your tower room —sorry about the intrusion, Nurse McCoy, but that corner of the house has the best view of the road in both directions."

"Never mind that. What did she do?"

Felix shrugged. "Just took a big carpet bag from where she'd stashed it in the willow bushes and set off on the road out of town."

"I always knew that hussy was a carpet-bagger! How long ago was that?"

Felix checked his watch. "A couple hours."

"Goll dumb it!" McCoy gave an angry kick to a rotting stump at the side of the trail. "I'll never catch up to her with that sort of head start!"

Ken frowned. "Why would you want to? I'd think you would be glad to be rid of her."

"To get back what she stole!"

Ken looked a little confused but comprehension dawned instantly on Felix's face. "I wondered earlier if you were thinking along those lines. I'll chase her down on my bike!" He turned to sprint up the hill.

McCoy stopped him. "And do what? Ask her nicely to give it back —as if she would! Or are you gonna search her yourself and have her scream bloody murder about a man assaulting a defenseless woman on the road?"

"So you chase her down and search her, Nurse McCoy." Ken told her. "She can't pull that sort of sham with a nurse —or if she does you just tell people she escaped from the county lunatic asylum and you have to bring her back."

"But with a two-hour lead—"

"Take Addie's trike. She won't mind, and I know she taught you how to ride it."

"Slower than a bike," Felix said dubiously.

"But faster than feet!" McCoy set off up the hill at a run.

***

Addie and Jacob had taught McCoy to ride Addie's tricycle as a marketing ploy for his cycle business to show everyone how easy it was. McCoy had never found it so all-fired easy, but she wasn't about to admit it. To her the tricycle was just a machine, and she wasn't going to be bested by no blamed machine. She'd gotten decent enough at maneuvering it to please Addie and Jacob; beyond that she left such things to folks who had time to fool about with them. However, when Ken had suggested she borrow Addie's tricycle to catch up to Esmerelda, McCoy had realized that instead of wasting her time, today the tricycle might prove her one chance of making up the time she had lost.

She pushed the bulky machine out of the carriage house, glared at it distrustfully, then sat down between the two big driving wheels. To get it going she had to shift almost her whole weight from one foot to the other on the pedals, then there was a bit of awkwardness while she reminded herself how to steer without pushing the mechanism too far and spinning in a circle. After a few false starts she got the feel of the machine again. As soon as she did she moved out onto the road and pumped away at the pedals as hard and as fast as she could. She was determined to overtake Esmerelda before the woman reached the crossroads at Four Corners. *If she gets there before me I won't have any way of knowing which direction she went —and then it's all over.*

McCoy came to a steep downhill and the tricycle started to run away with her. Her stomach leapt into her throat and she pulled on the brake with all her strength. The tricycle suddenly pitched her forward and there was a heart-stopping moment when she was convinced it would buck her off then run her over as it continued rolling back-over-front down the hill. Somehow, an insistent memory of Addie's instructions came to her aid, telling her to throw her weight backwards and ease up on the brake. She obeyed and the trike thunked back, its small stabilizing wheel hitting the ground again. Then the tricycle started to pick up speed again right away.

The whole ride down the hill was a series of nauseating lurches as she struggled to find the right balance with the brake. Too much force would wrench the machine to a stop, threatening to buck her off; too little would send both woman and tricycle flying downhill out of control.

McCoy remembered seeing Ken coasting his bicycle down hills with his legs up over his handlebars, looking as relaxed as if he'd been sitting on a porch swing. *And he has to keep balanced side-*

to-side on a bicycle! The thought flashed through McCoy's mind as she glanced at the madly spinning twin driving wheels that flanked her and kept the tricycle stable. *How in the Sam-hill does he do it?*

She didn't have time to ponder the question, but had to devote her full attention to controlling the machine's speed.

As soon as she reached the bottom of the slope, the road headed uphill again. Momentum carried her a short distance, then she had to pedal for all she was worth. Halfway up her strength gave out. She pulled on the brake to keep the tricycle from sliding backwards over her hard-earned distance, then got off and pushed.

*Let's hope there aren't any more hills like **that** on the way to Four Corners!*

She decided there couldn't be. Four Corners was a favorite destination of the local cycling club; Jacob and Addie rode there all the time. McCoy had to stretch her imagination to its absolute limit to picture Addie Kellam Simmons —that fragile little mite of a woman— even managing to negotiate this one terrifying set of hills on this machine, let alone any more of them. McCoy was certain the rest of the route must be level.

She crested the hill with a feeling of tremendous relief, sure that she'd conquered the hardest part of the road. Then she looked ahead and saw another downhill-uphill pairing virtually identical to the one she'd just conquered. Her heart fell, and her stomach plunked down on top of it.

McCoy started to develop a much deeper respect for Addie's abilities than she'd ever before possessed.

When she wasn't half-flying, half-jerk-stopping her way down hills (convinced of her own imminent death) or toiling her way up other hills that seemed endless, McCoy used her entire vocabulary of curses on the ruts in the road.

"Iffen I ever —" *THUNK!* "—get my hands—" *BUMP!* "—on the no good, lazy, son of a—" *THUNK! BUMP!! BAM! THUNK!!!* " —whose job it is to mend this road, I swear I'll—"

Here McCoy came to yet another hill and couldn't spare breath for grumbling.

After several more miles her nerves were frayed and her legs were like rubber. McCoy had always prided herself on her ability to work like an ox, but this type of work was entirely new to her. *And those club folks do this for **fun** —and come home happy as larks at the end of the day! Tiny little Addie more so than any of the rest of them!* If McCoy hadn't seen it herself many times, she wouldn't have credited the idea. She resolved to never dismiss dainty little Addie as weak, ever again.

Tired though she was, when McCoy saw a distant figure on the road up ahead she put on a fresh burst of speed. *Finally! Now I can deal with that woman and not have to cover any more miles on this confounded contraption except to get it home!*

If McCoy had caught up to Esmerelda on a downhill slope she'd have been sorely tempted to run her over, she was in such a foul mood by this point. As it was, Esmerelda had just started on an uphill grade when she happened to glance back. She stopped a moment, staring at the tricycle in astonishment. When she recognized McCoy she ran into the deep woods beside the trail.

McCoy groaned. The tricycle couldn't manage anything rougher than the road and the last thing she wanted to do right then was run. But she hadn't come this far to give up just as she'd spotted her quarry. She left the tricycle on the road and set out after Esmerelda in the closest approximation of a sprint that her rubbery legs could manage.

Luckily Esmerelda —who, after all, had walked as far as McCoy had cycled— was in even less of a condition for running. McCoy caught up to her after a few dozen yards and, with a sweeping kick which twinged her conscience not in the slightest, sent her sprawling to the ground. Esmerelda's hat came off as she hit the ground, along with a quantity of false hair. McCoy kicked the hat and sent it flying.

"I—" McCoy panted, "have had—" Esmerelda grabbed at her legs and tried to pull her to the ground. McCoy shook her off, then flipped her over with a well-placed boot. "—Enough—" Esmerelda yanked up a clod of dirt and flung it at her; McCoy grabbed both of her arms and pinned them behind her back, "—of you!"

Esmerelda made a ridiculous attempt at kicking that showed she'd never had brothers — leastways, none that could wrestle worth a hog's ear. McCoy thumped down on Esmerelda's legs to pin them to the ground, then with a tremendous yank tore the eyelet off the woman's own petticoat and hog-tied her with it. "I've got half a mind to leave you there like that!"

Esmerelda looked back towards the road and called out, "Help! Murder!"

"Oh, don't be a bigger fool than you already are!" McCoy tore another piece off Esmerelda's petticoat and gagged her with it.

Esmerelda squirmed, still trying to shout against the gag.

McCoy's hat had gotten knocked askew when she'd taken down Esmerelda. She stood and straightened it with a single, irritated jerk. "You keep up with that nonsense and I really will leave you here, you hear? There's bears and mountain lions in these woods, you think you can sweet-talk them?"

Esmerelda stopped squirming and lay quiet.

"That's better." McCoy took the gag out of Esmerelda's mouth. "Now, you've got something that don't belong to you."

Esmerelda looked surprised. Then she glared at McCoy. "Is that why you chased me down?" She gave a scornful laugh. "Well, it doesn't belong to you, either."

"No, but I know who it does." McCoy grabbed Esmerelda's carpet bag from where it had fallen when she'd knocked the woman to the ground. She unlatched it and spilled its contents over the forest floor. Small pots of powder and paint went rolling and bouncing over the soft carpet of soil and fir needles, hiding themselves under sword ferns and falling down holes in the ground.

"Why should you care?" Scoffed Esmerelda. Then she laughed. "Don't tell me *you're* sweet on that bumbling fool of a—"

McCoy stuffed the gag back in Esmerelda's mouth. "He's in my charge, and that's all that matters."

She found what she'd come for, then re-tied Esmerelda's bonds more loosely. "There now," she told her, suddenly in a much better mood. "Shouldn't take you more than twenty or thirty minutes to wriggle out of that. Just remember the mountain lions and don't lose no time about it."

Esmerelda tried to shout something but the gag was still in her mouth.

"No need to thank me," McCoy told her calmly. Then she leaned over Esmerelda and gave her the most menacing look possible. "But if you ever come near someone in my charge again, then next time I will leave you for the mountain lions, you hear?"

Esmerelda glared at her. McCoy straightened, grinned, and walked away.

***

The ride home was much easier than the ride out had been.

Afterword

Jacob and Addie had passed a lovely honeymoon. As they faced the last leg of their journey back to Chetzemoka they shared a slight sadness that this sweet time should be over, but it was well-tempered by their excitement to be returning home to a new life together.

"It was very generous of your uncle Silas to pay for our train tickets out to New York," Addie told Jacob as she re-packed their bags after a few days' stop in San Francisco.

He smiled. "Well, it was important to him that my mother get a chance to meet you."

"I liked your mother a lot —your father, too."

"I'm very glad."

Addie folded a pair of her silk pantalets and tucked them into a corner of her crowded suitcase. "I should send your mother some silk next time my pa's ship comes back from the Orient. He always bring my mother and me far more than we can use."

He smiled at her and handed her the silk petticoat she'd brought on the trip but wasn't wearing for travel. "I'm sure she'd appreciate that." A yawn caught him off-guard. "Oh, excuse me!"

Addie giggled at him. "It was a long trip across the country, wasn't it?"

"Definitely! It was nice of your parents' friends to let us stay with them here in San Francisco a few days so we didn't have to rush straight from the train to the steamer." He handed her a box of candies their hosts had given them to bring back to Addie's mother. "If we ever do a trip like this again, the

Northern Pacific Line is supposed to finally get all its pieces connected up by the end of next year. If they manage it we'd be able to take a train all the way to Tacoma without a big detour south like we did this time."

Addie found room for the candies then shrugged and closed the suitcase. "The railroads have been trying to connect up their northern routes for years. I'll believe it when I see it. Besides, it was nice to see San Francisco again. Ken and I were born here, you know."

"You told me that." He took the heavy suitcase from her. "How old did you say you were when your family moved to Chetzemoka?"

"I was twelve and Ken was eleven. We moved up there when Pa got command of his first Trans-Pacific ship."

She put on her hat and flashed Jacob a mischievous grin in the mirror as she slid her hatpins in place. "I suspect the real reason you wish that the Northern Pacific would hurry and finish is because you got so seasick on the steamer from Chetzemoka on the start of our trip. I think you're afraid it's going to happen again on the way back."

"Perhaps..." He admitted sheepishly.

Addie laughed. Then she turned to face her husband, put her arms around his torso and gazed up at him. "I always told my mother I didn't want to marry a sailor, but I don't think she ever dreamed I'd fall in love with a man who gets sick at the sight of his own washbasin!"

"Oh, come now! I'm not that bad!"

She stood on tip-toes and pulled his shoulders down so she could kiss him. "I'd still have married you, even if you were."

They made it to the docks without incident and looked for the ship that would take them back home to Chetzemoka. Another ship at the same dock happened to be unloading passengers from Port Angeles nearby; as they passed through the disembarking crowds a certain face in the throng caught Jacob's attention. He started and a name escaped his mouth involuntarily. "Eunice?"

The woman —a tall brunette with pale skin and large brown eyes— looked up in surprise.

Addie gazed quizzically at Jacob. She wondered who this woman was, but more importantly she was curious as to why her husband knew this Eunice by her Christian name.

When Eunice saw Jacob a sly smile of recognition spread over her features. "Why, Jacob Simmons!" She purred, then undulated through the crowd towards them.

Jacob's face turned into a patchwork of pallor and scarlet. He looked as though he regretted recognizing the woman —profoundly regretted it.

Addie whispered, "Who is she?"

Jacob didn't answer. He just put a hand protectively on Addie's shoulder.

Eunice reached them and Addie was nearly bowled over by the reek of patchouly emanating from the woman. *Pee-ew! That's worse than the time Pa's ship transported a whole load of India shawls! Mother made him sleep in the spare room his first night of shore leave when he got home, and none of the rest of us blamed her.*

Eunice favored Jacob with a sensuous smile. She paid less attention to Addie than she might a pet dog. "How are you, Jacob?"

Jacob seemed excruciatingly uncomfortable. "It's been a long time."

"A very long time." Eunice moved shockingly close.

Jacob cleared his throat. "Allow me to introduce my *wife*, **Mrs.** Adora *Simmons*." He emphasized the matrimonial portions of the introduction.

Addie inclined her head towards Eunice. The woman's eyes flashed venom at her.

Jacob continued, "Adora, this is Miss Eunice Nettleton. Or is it Mrs. Skinem now?"

Eunice gave a short, derisive laugh. "Jacob, why would you think such a thing?"

"Well, you ran o—" Jacob stopped himself, then squared his shoulders. "You were very friendly with Charlie Skinem and his spiritualist friends."

Eunice smiled on one corner of her mouth. "I suppose I was. Very friendly."

Her wicked expression shocked Addie speechless.

Jacob went on, "Just after you lost contact with me, wasn't it, Miss Nettleton?"

"'After?'" Eunice smirked. "Yes, I suppose you would tell yourself that. You were always so ingenuous, Jacob. Not that you didn't have some redeeming qualities." She let her eyes linger over his muscular form.

Addie, who'd had quite enough of this, cleared her throat and took a possessive hold of Jacob's hand. "Dearest, shouldn't we be getting aboard the steamer?" She glared over at the Nettleton creature. "We've had such a lovely honeymoon, but I'm looking forward to seeing all our friends at home again."

"Absolutely!" Jacob squeezed Addie's hand and started to go. Then he paused and looked back at Eunice. "Miss Nettleton?"

She shot Addie a triumphant look. "Yes, Jacob?"

"At the same time you —lost touch with me and got so friendly with Charlie Skinem, something went missing that I'd like to have back."

"Why, Jacob!" She strutted close to him, smiling that same sensuous smile again. "I had no idea you felt that way!"

He shook her off with a disgusted expression. "You know very well what I'm referring to. It can't possibly have any value to you, but it meant a great deal to me. If you still have it—"

"I don't." She dropped the affectation of sensuality and stood there, a vulgar, uncouth woman reeking of patchouly. "As you said, it had no value to me and it would have been too much trouble to keep it. Good-bye, Mr. Simmons." She turned away, giving her head that peculiarly ludicrous inclination that all women affect when they are particularly anxious to be noticed, but also particularly anxious to not have it noticed that they wish to be noticed.

Jacob didn't wait for her disappear into the crowd before he turned away. He simply pressed

Addie's hand and went up the gangplank with his wife. "I'm very sorry about that."

Addie raised a suspicious eyebrow at him. "What was that all about, Jacob?"

"An embarrassing episode I would prefer to forget."

Addie stopped, looked askance at her husband, peered back in the direction Eunice had disappeared, then faced Jacob again with an affronted expression. "That *creature?!* Oh, Jacob—!"

"Please don't beleaguer the point, Addie. I guarantee you can't possibly give me a harsher lecture on the idiocy of young men than I've given myself many times over. But it was five years ago —long before I met you." He kissed Addie's hand. "So don't worry. Please?"

They reached the deck of the steamer and Addie frowned petulantly.

Jacob stroked her cheek, not caring about the crowds of people around them. After a moment she gave him the very faintest of smiles.

"I'm all yours now, I promise." He raised her hand again and kissed her wedding ring this time. "That's what this means."

She pressed her hand against his cheek and smiled more confidently.

When they were settled in deck chairs with their travel rugs over their laps, Addie turned to Jacob. "You said something went missing that meant a lot to you. What were you talking about?"

Jacob sighed and glanced back towards the dock with an angry expression. "She stole my diary. It had over a year's worth of entries in it —most of them having nothing at all to do with her, since the book was already more than two-thirds full when I made her acquaintance. That earlier portion is what I really minded losing: it covered the last few months my grandparents were alive. The last few letters my grandmother ever wrote to me were tucked into that diary, too."

"Oh, Jacob!" Addie pressed his hand. "I'm so sorry!"

He shook his head. "I wish she hadn't thrown it away. I think that diary would mean even more to me now than when she took it; besides my last memories of my grandparents, it also covered Uncle Silas' visit to New York six years ago." Jacob smiled wryly to himself. "Since I moved to Chetzemoka, there've been a number of times I've wished I could look back on my impressions of Uncle Silas when I was nineteen and compare them to the way I see him now, and think about how much I've grown."

"My dear Jacob…" Addie gazed at him with love and sympathy in her eyes, and rested her hand on his cheek.

He smiled at her. "So you see how dreadful Miss Nettleton is, and why you have nothing to worry about?"

Addie nodded. "I do, my love." She drew Jacob's hand into her lap and together they watched the dock grow smaller as the ship moved out onto the water, bringing them homewards.

When enough time and scenery had passed for their minds to shift to other topics, Jacob asked Addie what she supposed everyone in Chetzemoka had been up to while they were gone.

She smiled. "Based on Ken's reactions to some illustrations he saw in an issue of *Illustrated Sporting and Dramatic News*, I'm guessing we'll get home to find my brother either able to do some spectacular new tricks on his bike, or else with some spectacularly broken bones. If he'd killed himself Mother would have telegraphed us."

"Give him some credit, Addie!" Jacob couldn't help chuckling but he tried to look serious. "He and Felix are the best riders in the club."

"Yes, but Ken takes more headers than the rest of the club put together."

"Only because he tries to do things the rest of us know would end disastrously if we attempted them. I'm surprised he does so well most of the time."

"He's got our pa's sense of balance and our mother's conviction that failure is just a step on the road to success."

Jacob laughed and nodded. He watched the shore passing for a while then mused, "I wonder if that stray cat I was trying to make friends with is still prowling around Uncle Silas' house."

Addie perked up excitedly. "A cat?"

Jacob nodded. "I think she wandered up from the waterfront. She's probably an old ship's cat who decided to retire to land. I got her to the point where she'd come in the kitchen."

"Oh, I hope it's still around when we get home! I truly like cats!"

Jacob smiled at his wife's enthusiasm. "Well, we'll make sure we get one then, one way or another."

Addie beamed. She snuggled closer to Jacob over the arms of their chairs.

After a while he told her, "I think Mrs. Brown and the doctor will have some news for everyone by the time we get home."

"Hmm? Why do you say that —what kind of news?"

"Well, I saw Nurse McCoy knitting baby stockings. I can't imagine who else they could be for, can you?"

Addie's eyes got big. "Oh, I'm sure you're right! How clever of Nurse McCoy!"

Jacob nodded.

Addie went on, "Speaking of knitting, I hope your uncle Silas likes that muffler your mother sent back with us."

"Uncle Silas would like anything Mother made for him." Jacob stretched out his legs. "I wonder how he's been while we've been gone."

Addie stretched her own dainty legs, then shook out her skirt. "Of all our friends and family back in Chetzemoka, I think your Uncle Silas is the one we should worry about the least."

Jacob frowned in surprise. "Why do you say that?"

Addie smiled. "Because he's had Nurse McCoy looking after him! She wouldn't let trouble come within a mile of someone in her charge —not without giving that trouble the kicking of its life! I deeply pity anyone foolish enough to get between Nurse McCoy and one of her patients."

Jacob grinned at his wife and nodded agreement. "So do I, Addie. So do I!"

***

When they got home the news was all about Kitty Brown's expectant condition and Ken's dislocated elbow. Jacob and Addie privately chuckled at how close they'd hit the mark with their speculations on the steamer. Beyond these two big pieces of news, Silas and Nurse McCoy told them nothing of consequence had happened while they were gone.

After they'd sat visiting a while and filled Silas in on all the news from New York, Addie started to droop in her chair, exhausted from their long journey.

McCoy set down her knitting. "You want me to get dinner started for y'all?"

Addie's head shot up. "Oh, no! Please, I've been so looking forward to trying out that big, beautiful kitchen!"

McCoy chuckled. "It's all yours. You're in charge now." She resumed her knitting, then stopped suddenly. "But I cook your uncle's food, mind?"

Jacob felt relieved that his dear Addie wouldn't be expected to cater to Silas' dyspeptic whims.

"Alright," she agreed. "But who cooks for you, Hettie?"

"I do, of course. And the name's McCoy."

Addie looked slightly disappointed. "Don't you think you might try my cooking once in a while?"

"Ain't my place."

"But, if I made extra?" Addie asked softly.

McCoy just shook her head and kept on knitting.

Addie's face fell. "I'm not bad at cooking, really…"

Silas motioned Addie over to him and whispered something to her. Her expression brightened and she stood up straighter.

She lifted her arms in a theatrical gesture of importance and told McCoy in a mock-imperious tone, "I, Mrs. Adora Simmons, mistress of this household, am ordering you to eat my cooking!" She dropped her arms again, blushing. "That is," she added shyly. "—When you want to, and when I fix something you think you might like."

McCoy allowed herself a small smile. "Alright, then."

Addie beamed triumphantly, then rushed upstairs to change out of her travelling clothes.

Jacob stayed downstairs long enough to enjoy the radiant expression on Addie's face as she came back down and took control of her own kitchen for the very first time. Then he went upstairs so he, too, could change out of his travelling clothes.

Things in his room weren't quite where he had left them. Addie had folded her travelling dress and laid it on his bed —their bed, now, he realized. He felt a thrill of love and pride at the sight of this dainty feminine touch entering his life.

He wasn't surprised to find his wash set moved and his cycling magazines out of order: Silas had told him about Ken staying here after he'd broken his arm, and he didn't mind in the slightest. He was surprised, though, to see a new book on his bookshelf.

It stood out very obviously because instead of being neatly lined up like the rest of them, it was crammed in on top of his diaries, laying over the other volumes. At first Jacob thought it might be one of his bound collection of cycling magazines that Ken had perused and then casually thrown back inside the glass-fronted case, but closer inspection showed it wasn't.

That's funny... Jacob opened the case and took out the extra book. As soon as his hand touched the cover a thrill of suspected recognition shot through him and his heart started racing. *It can't possibly be!*

He remembered seeing Eunice coming off of the Port Angeles steamer.

Could— Possibly—?

He opened the cover and read, in his own handwriting,

Jacob B. Simmons

"It is a great advance in civilization to be able to describe the common facts of life, and...at least an equal advance to wish to describe them."

Private diary from March 12, 1876—

He sat down heavily on his desk chair. *How on Earth—?*

He heard footsteps at the door to his room. Looking over, he saw Nurse McCoy.

"Your missus wants to know if you want a cream soup or a clear one."

Jacob was so overcome by astonishment at finding his lost diary he couldn't answer the question. He just stared blankly at Nurse McCoy.

"Now, if you ask me it's all a question of digestion. There's some people can digest cream soups, and some can't—"

"Nurse McCoy—" Jacob interrupted, then stared dumbly at her. Finally he asked, "Are you sure nothing happened while we were gone?"

She shrugged. "Nothin' worth talking about."

He pointed at the diary. "But this!"

She shrugged again. "I don't abide people stealing from folks in my charge."

Jacob just stared at her.

Seeing that he wasn't quite comprehending, she added, "You're in my charge. All this family is."

He was almost overcome with emotion. "I don't know how to thank you. I don't even know how you did it—"

"Never mind that. Best way to thank me is just make sure your uncle keeps paying my wages on time. Now, do you want cream soup or clear?"

"I— uh, cream, I guess."

"I figured you'd be that sort." She turned to go, then stopped suddenly. "Oh, and by the way?"

"Yes?"

"You might want to start taking your uncle's advice about locking your desk."

Appendices

Appendix I: Recipes

Appendix II: Victorian Nurses and the Origins of Nurse McCoy

Appendix III: Sources related to Victorian medicine

Appendix IV: Fraudulent Spiritualists and Esmerelda's Tricks

Appendix V: Bon Mots

Appendix VI: Marriage, Breach of Promise Suits

Appendix VII: Notes on Victorian Cycling

Appendix VIII: Miscellaneous Notes

Appendix I
Recipes

N.B. Historic recipes tend to be based on much smaller eggs than the ones typically sold in modern supermarkets. If small eggs (as from bantam chickens) are unavailable, remember to reduce the quantities of eggs when making historic recipes.

Recipes appear in the order in which the foods appeared in the story:

Invalid foods
Tamarind water
Cream of Rice
Stewed Prunes
Beef tea
Panada

Non-invalid foods
Coasting cookies
Southern corn bread
Sallie Lunn

Further food-related notes

Nineteenth-century nurses acted as nutritionists for their patients (among their many other duties), and understanding the role diet plays in health was an important part of their job. Nurse McCoy would have learned specific recipes for invalid foods while she was in nursing school and kept a book of them. The following are authentic nineteenth-century recipes for invalid foods:

Tamarind water

The Queen of the Household, by Mrs. M.W. Ellsworth, Ellsworth & Brey: Detroit, 1899, p. 619.

Put tamarinds into a pitcher or tumbler till it is 1/4 to 1/3 full; then fill up with cold water, cover it, and let it infuse for 1/2 hour or more.

***

Cream of rice

The Queen of the Household [ibid.] p. 629.

Cream of rice is a dainty dish to set before the king, or greater than the king, a convalescent friend. Things taste better for coming in unexpectedly, and the friends of invalids do well to rack their brains for some pretty novelty to waken appetite or restore exhausted strength. To make the cream of rice, boil the uncooked breast of a fowl and a cup of rice in chicken broth until soft enough to rub through a fine sieve; thin the paste thus formed with boiling milk, seasoned with salt, pepper and nutmeg to the consistency of thick cream.

***

Stewed prunes

Food For The Invalid: The Convalescent; the Dyspeptic; and the Gouty by J. Milner Fothergill, M.D. New York: MacMillan and Co., 1880, p. 63.

Wash the fruit, and for every pound allow half a pound of raw sugar and one pint of water. Boil the sugar and water together for ten minutes, then put in the fruit, and let it boil gently for two hours, or until perfectly tender, so that it breaks if touched with the finger. Drain the syrup from the prunes, and boil it until it becomes thick, then put the prunes back into it, and let them stand until the next day."

***

Beef tea
The Capitol Cook Book Chicago: The Werner Company, 1896. p. 411.

One pound of *lean* beaf, cut into small pieces. Put into a glass canning-jar without a drop of water; cover tightly, and set in a pot of cold water. Heat gradually to a boil, and continue this steadily for three or four hours, until the meat is like white rags, and the juice all drawn out. Season with salt to taste, and when cold, skim.

***

Panada
In the Kitchen by Elizabeth S. Miller, Boston: Lee & Shepard, 1875, p. 533.

Grated bread or rolled crackers may be used. To one ounce of bread add half a pint of boiling water, let it boil a few minutes, then sweeten with loaf sugar and flavor with wine and nutmeg.

***

Non-invalid recipes for foods that appear elsewhere in the story:

Coasting Cookies
Elizabeth S. Miller. *In the Kitchen*, Boston: Lee & Shepard, 1875, p. 365.
One pound of flour.
Eight ounces of butter.
Half a pint of molasses.
One tablespoonful of soda, beaten very hard in the molasses.
One tablespoonful of coriander seed, and one of carraway [sic], pounded in a mortar.
Ginger to taste.
Soften the butter, stir in the molasses, ginger, seeds, and flour; roll thin, cut, and bake in a quick oven.

Southern Corn Bread
Woman's Exchange Cookbook. Late 19th-century, p. 71.
Take 3 cups of corn meal, the white is preferable, 1 cup of flour, 1 tablepoonful of sugar, 1 tablespoonful of butter, 1 teaspoonful of salt, 3 eggs, 2 cups of milk and 2 heaping teaspoonfuls of baking powder.
Thoroughly sift together the flour and corn meal and stir in the sugar and salt, rub in the butter, beat the eggs thoroughly then add them and the milk, lastly

put in the baking powder and mix with a spoon to a stiff batter; pour into well greased pans and bake quickly. This is a nice receipt and the quicker it is put together the lighter and nicer it will be.

Sally Lunn
Woman's Exchange Cookbook. Late 19th-century, p. 79.
This cake was formerly used on Southern tables only, but is now a favorite in all sections. Is easily made and inexpensive.

Warm one-half cup of butter in a pint of milk, add a teaspoonful of salt, same of sugar and one-half pint of flour[*]. Beat thoroughly, then add three well beaten eggs. Lastly, add half a cup of home made yeast. Beat thoroughly again, set to rise over night. In the morning dissolve half a teaspoonful of soda in a little warm water and stir in the batter; then turn into well buttered tins, let rise again twenty minutes and bake in a quick oven. The cakes should be torn apart, not cut. Dust the top while warm with pulverized sugar. Delicious with breakfast.

*I'm quite convinced that a printer's error was responsible for the original of this recipe only calling for "one-half pint of flour." Considering it takes twice that much milk, and three eggs as well, such a small quantity of flour seems more appropriate to a pudding than a cake. I used 1 1/2 pints flour —i.e., 3 cups.

Further food-related notes:

—Tabasco sauce dates back to the 1860s. There were many other hot sauces (i.e. pepper sauces) available in the nineteenth-century, but Tabasco has had the most staying power as a brand.

—In the nineteenth-century, "refrigerator" was the most common term for the appliance now more usually called an ice box. For more on this, see the article "Ice Boxes vs. Refrigerators" by Jonathan Rees: http://histsociety.blogspot.com/2013/12/iceboxes-vs-refrigerators.html For a description of living with a Victorian refrigerator, see http://www.thisvictorianlife.com/kitchen-and-dining-room.html

Appendix II
Victorian Nurses and the Origins of Nurse McCoy

In the mid-nineteenth-century, when various careers were becoming increasingly formalized, a massive shift occured in how people saw nursing. In the twenty-first century, if someone were asked to describe qualities that make a good nurse, they might list kindness, patience, generosity, and a strong work ethic. At the start of the nineteenth-century, however, public opinion of nurses was very different. A Victorian nurse reported, "When I first began my hospital training, hospital nursing was thought to be a profession which no decent woman of any rank could follow. If a servant turned nurse, it was supposed she did so because she had lost her character. We have changed all that now."[1] By the time of the interview nurses were held in quite high esteem, their image being very similar the present one. The Victorian nurse who witnessed these changes credited them entirely to Florence Nightingale, the "Queen of Nurses"[2].

In 1818, two years before Nightingale's birth, the

---

[1] Alldridge, Lizzie, *Great Men and Famous Women*, Ed. Charles F. Horne, New York: Selmar Press, 1894, p. 369.

[2] Tooley, Sarah A., *The Life of Florence Nightingale*, New York: Cassell and Company, 1910.

poor reputation of nurses in the English-speaking world was embodied by a minor character in Mary Shelley's novel *Frankenstein*: "The sound disturbed an old woman who was sleeping in a chair beside me. She was a hired nurse, the wife of one of the turnkeys, and her countenance expressed all those bad qualities which often characterize that class. The lines of her face were hard and rude, like that of persons accustomed to see without sympathizing in sights of misery. Her tone expressed her entire indifference…" A charity hospital in New York before the organization of a nursing school there was described in ghastly terms: "In the fever ward (forty beds) the only nurse was a woman from the workhouse, under a six-month sentence for drunkenness."[3]

As a young woman Nightingale realized the inadequacy of many women who called themselves nurses. In 1845 she wrote, "I saw a poor woman die before my eyes this summer, because there was no one but fools to sit up with her, who poisoned her as much as if they had given her arsenic."[4] Her attitude against improper nursing remained constant, and in her book *Notes on Nursing* Nightingale boldly declared, "If a patient is cold, if a patient is feverish, if a patient is faint, if he is sick after taking food, if he has a bed-sore, it is generally the fault not of the

---

[3] "Occupations for Women: The Trained Nurse." P.G. Hubert Jr., *The Woman's Book: Volume I*, New York: Charles Scribner's Sons, 1894, p. 36.
[4] Hall, Eleanor Francis. *Florence Nightingale.* New York: The MacMillan Company, 1920, p. 49.

disease, but of the nursing... I use the word nursing for want of a better. It has been limited to signify little more than the administration of medicines and the application of poultices. It ought to signify the proper use of fresh air, light, warmth, cleanliness, quiet, and the proper selection and administration of diet..."[5]

At this time, medicine in general was becoming increasingly professionalized. In 1858 the British General Medical Council officially began differentiating between "qualified" and "unqualified" practitioners. The United States had only four medical colleges in 1800, but by 1877 this number had swelled to seventy-three.[6] The American Medical Association was organized in 1847[7] (seven years before Nightingale made her famous departure to serve as a nurse in the Crimean War), and between 1864 and 1902 another fifteen specialty medical groups appeared in the U.S. [8]

Nightingale was the daughter of a wealthy squire[9],

---

[5] Nightingale, Florence, *Notes on Nursing: What It Is, and What It Is Not.*, London: Harrison and Sons, 1860. p. 2.

[6] "Physicians, science, and status: issues in the professionalization of Anglo-American medicine in the nineteenth century.", Shortt, S.E., *Medical History*, January, 1983, 27 (1): 51—68. <https://www.ncbi.nlm.nih.gov/pmc/articles/PMC1139264/>

[7] Shortt, ibid.

[8] Shortt, ibid.

[9] "Florence Nightingale.", Frances J. Dyer, *The*

yet despite nursing's vulgar reputation she felt herself drawn to caregiving. Starting in 1844 Nightingale examined conditions in both civil and military hospitals all over Europe. Paid nurses, as described above, were looked on very poorly when Nightingale was a young woman but religious orders who provided healthcare were accorded respect. It was to these Sisters that Nightingale looked for guidance and training. She received training in health-care practices from Protestant Deaconesses in Kaiserswerth (in what is now Germany), and with the Catholic Sisters of St. Vincent De Paul in Paris.[10]

When Nightingale returned to England she took over management of a London Sanitarium for Governesses[11]. But it was her work nursing soldiers in the Crimean War that made her name a household word.

Conditions in British military hospitals on the Crimean front in 1854 were described in hellish terms: "miles of fetid and over-crowded corridors, without proper beds and bedding, without proper food, medicine, or attendance, and above all, without the means of breathing fresh air."[12]   Besides wounds received in actual battle, the soldiers were suffering

Congregationalist, May 9, 1895, p. 716.
[10] "Florence Nightingale." *Chambers's Encyclopedia*, Vol. 5, New York: Collier, 1890. p. 599.
[11] "Florence Nightingale." *The Chicago Medical Journal*, June, 1860, p. 374.
[12] "Something of What Florence Nightingale Has Done and Is Doing." *The St. James Magazine*, London: W. Kent & Co., 1861, p. 32.

frostbite, scurvy, dysentery, camp fever and cholera.[13]
The infectious cases were jumbled indiscriminately
with the men who had open wounds, and lack of
sufficient caregivers resulted in a situation
where injuries went undressed for five or six days and
wounds became clogged with maggots.[14]

Britain's Secretary of War, who "knew that a
woman's hand and brain was needed at the Crimea"[15],
wrote to Nightingale asking her to take charge of
nursing on the Crimean front and improve the
situation. She, having heard of the conditions, had
already written to the same Secretary of War asking
permission for this very duty, and their letters crossed
in the mail[16]. She left for the war on October 21,
1854. The small group of women who accompanied
her in this endeavor had been carefully chosen for
their characters as well as proven abilities to care for
the sick: they included the daughter of a bishop, ten
Roman Catholic Sisters of Mercy, and ten Protestant
Sisters, and a few carefully chosen lay nurses.

They brought portable cooking stoves[17] with them,
which immediately upon arrival were put to use
producing nourishing food for the starving patients.
Within a week they established a separate kitchen

---

[13] "Florence Nightingale: An Address to Nurses."
W.C. Cahall, M.D., *The Philadelphia Medical
Journal*, June 6, 1902, p. 977.
[14] Cahall, ibid.
[15] "Florence Nightingale." *The Unitarian.*, February,
1890, p. 99.
[16] *Chambers's Encyclopedia*, ibid.
[17] *The St. James Magazine*, ibid., p. 33.

and engaged civilian cooks, at which point Nightingale's nurses could more thoroughly devote themselves to the vital task of sanitation. They raised private funds to build baths, wash-houses, and additional kitchens.

Nightingale would be on her feet for twenty hours at a time[18]. When bureaucratic red tape failed to provide requisition orders for needed materials, she simply commanded the male orderlies to break into the warehouse[19] and took out the necessary supplies.

Under Nightingale's supervision, mortality in British military hospitals on the Crimean front was reported to drop from sixty percent to only a little over one percent[20]. The soldiers, many of whom were from humble backgrounds, were so in awe of this high-born noblewoman and her tender care of the suffering that they wrote home about kissing her shadow[21] when she came close to them.

The presence of an aristocratic lady elevated the morals of the men at the same time she ministered to their physical needs. One man reported, "Before Miss Nightingale came, there was such cussin' and swearing', and after that it was as holy as a church."[22]

When Nightingale returned to England from the Crimea, she used donated funds to start the first

---

[18] *Chambers's Encyclopedia*, ibid.

[19] *The Philadelphia Medical Journal*, ibid.

[20] *The Unitarian*, ibid.

[21] Cahall, ibid., p. 978.

[22] *Pictorial History of the Russian War: 1854-5-6 With Maps, Plans, and Wood Engravings.* London: W. & R. Chambers., 1856, p. 508.

English training school for nurses, which opened in 1860[23].

Formal training brought about what was later termed a "transformation" in nursing, with the new *trained* nurse characterized by "her neat uniform, her eternal vigilance concerning neatness, order and cleanliness, and her methodical system of work."[24]

Nightingale was British, but her work impacted — and was appreciated by— people around the world. Her paper "Life or Death in India" was read at the Meeting of the National Association for Social Science in Norwich, 1873 and a few years later *Chambers's Encyclopaedia* called it "one of the most remarkable public papers ever penned." In the 1880s many American girls were required to memorize and recite a Longfellow poem written in honor of Nightingale:

> Whene'er a noble deed is wrought,
> Whene'er is spoken a noble thought,
> Our hearts, in glad surprise,
> To higher levels rise.
>
> The tidal wave of deeper souls
> Into our inmost being rolls,
> And lifts us unawares
> Out of meaner cares.
>
> Honor to those whose words or deeds
> Thus help us in our daily needs,
> And by their overflow

---

[23] *The Woman's Book*, ibid.
[24] *The Woman's Book*, ibid.

Raise us from what is low!

Thus thought I, as by night I read
Of the great army of the dead,
The trenches cold and damp,
The starved and frozen camp,--

The wounded from the battle-plain
In dreary hospitals of pain,
The cheerless corridors,
The cold and stony floors.

Lo! in that house of misery,
A lady with a lamp I see
Pass through the glimmering gloom,
And flit from room to room.

And slow, as in a dream of bliss,
The speechless sufferer turns to kiss
Her shadow, as it falls
Upon the darkening walls.

As if a door in heaven should be
Opened and then closed suddenly,
The vision came and went,
The light shone and was spent.

On England's annals, through the long
Hereafter of her speech and song,
That light its rays shall cast
From portals of the past.

A Lady with a Lamp shall stand

In the great history of the land,
A noble type of good,
Heroic womanhood.

Nor even shall be wanting here
The palm, the lily, and the spear;
The symbols that of yore
Santa Filomena bore.[25]

Thanks to Florence Nightingale (and the publicity which had surrounded her work), the public's image of a nurse had changed from a picture of an indifferent jailer's wife to a saintly Lady With A Lamp bringing enlightenment and hope to the suffering.

Nightingale's name became synonymous with kind, dutiful nursing. Clara Barton, the Civil War nurse who founded the American Red Cross, was called "The American Florence Nightingale", and she shared one of Nightingale's nicknames, "The Angel of the Battlefield"[26].

Nightingale's training school for nurses in London inspired similar institutions in the U.S. In 1873[27] the New England Hospital in Boston gave the first official nursing diploma earned by an American to a

---

[25] *Bancroft's Fifth Reader*, A.L. Bancroft, 1883. pp. 237-238.
[26] "Clara Barton: Angel of the Battlefied." *American Leaders: Book Two*, Walter Lefferts, Ph.D. Philadelphia: J. B. Lippincott Company, 1919. p. 311.
[27] *The Woman's Book*, ibid.

Miss Richards, and Belleview Hospital in New York opened a training school the same year. By 1883 there were seventeen training schools for nurses in the United States, and applicants were examined for physical stamina as well as intelligence. Students accepted to these nursing schools received their board and lodging free of expense, and after a initial trial period (one to three months, depending on the school) had been completed they received a regular salary as well.[28] In most schools this salary increased as the student progressed in school. The fact that nursing students were paid, whereas studying to become a doctor was (and still is) a very expensive undertaking accounted for much larger numbers of women studying to be nurses than to become doctors.

 Besides her salary, free room and board, any student who fell ill during her two years of nursing school was given free health care. All these things added up to make the occupation a tempting one: by 1894 the U.S. had nearly two hundred schools for nurses.[29]

After her schooling was completed, a trained nurse could "command her own price, and that price will depend upon the wealth and liberality of her patrons, and the ability which she brings to bear on the case in hand. Good nursing is very often more important than good doctoring, and thousands of people are willing to pay liberally for such exceptional help."[30]

---

[28] "Professional Nursing." George J. Manson, *Work for Women*, G.P. New York: Putnam's Sons, 1883, pp. 47—59.

[29] *The Woman's Book*, ibid, p. 39.

To proponents of the new style of nursing, education was vital. Nightingale herself would eventually take a stand against official state registration for nurses, partly because she felt the proposed requirements were not strong enough.[31] However, she never altered her belief that nurses should have the best education available to aid them in caring for their patients.

Some have defended the reputations of women whose caregiving were self-taught and who therefore align more appropriately with what might be termed "pre-Nightingale" nursing. One example is Mary Seacole, who ran a 'British hotel' at Balaclava during the Crimean War. Historian A.N. Wilson described the situation in the following terms, "Miss Nightingale's hospital was where you were taken if you were wounded or fell sick. Mary Seacole was on hand for the troops in the long months when nothing appeared to be happening and … she showed courage under fire."[32] Even when lacking in formal training, traditional nurses like Seacole could still embody the same devotion to care which characterized Nightingale. Perhaps the best words to

---

[30] Manson, ibid, p. 58.

[31] Helmstadter, Carol. "Florence Nightingale's Opposition to State Registration for Nurses." *Nursing History Review.* <https://www.questia.com/library/journal/1P3-1394543641/florence-nightingale-s-opposition-to-state-registration>

[32] Wilson, *The Victorians*. New York: W.W. Norton & Co. 2003, p. 178.

use in association with Seacole would be gumption and grit. In her memoir she described her own determination to help those on the front: "Let what might happen, to the Crimea I would go. If in no other way, then I would upon my own responsibility and at my own cost."[33] Her 1881 obituary in *The Englishwoman's Review* recalled her heroism during the war, reporting, "She was present at many battles, and at the risk of her life often conveyed the wounded off the field."[34]

In certain circles controversy has arisen over recognition of figures like Seacole. Those who like their history one-sided and simple seem to feel that the only way to laud Seacole involves demonizing Nightingale, and naturally Nightingale's defenders take issue with this.[35] Personally, I like to think history is big enough to recognize all its heroines.

When my husband Gabriel was helping me brainstorm ideas for a trained nurse for my historical fiction series, we wanted a character who would

---

[33] Seacole, Mary. *Wonderful Adventures of Mrs. Seacole in Many Lands.* New York: Oxford University Press, 1988, p. 80.

[34] "Death of Mrs. Mary Seacole." *Englishwoman's Review*, June 15, 1881, p. 278.

[35] McDonald, Professor Lynn. "Lessons in lies: How the BBC, school text books and even exam boards have twisted history to smear Florence Nightingale and make a saint of this woman", *Daily Mail*, July 31, 2014. <https://www.dailymail.co.uk/femail/article-2712683/Mary-Seacole-saint-Florence-Nightingake-smeared-twisting-history.html>

bridge the gaps between all these images and embody the full heritage of Victorian nursing history: someone who had the highly capable attributes of a Nightingale nurse, but who had the rough edges of her predecessors; a woman who'd learned homeopathic remedies from her mother and grandmother the way Mary Seacole and countless women throughout the ages have done, but who also had strict, formal training and was fiercely proud of the fact.

Since the nurse in my series was to be a caregiver and complement to Silas Hayes, a cantankerous hypochondriac, she had to be a match for him in pure cussedness and also provide a commensurate level of comic relief. Following the tropes of various serialized nineteenth-century fiction (and the likely socioeconomic origins of a woman who went into nursing school) indicated a character with a fairly strong ethnic background. My first thought was that she might be Irish, but Gabriel and I both felt that this was a little too much of a cliché, and he was the one who suggested Appalachian. (Fans of *A Rapping At the Door* will remember that McCoy did have an Irish mentor, Matron O'Reilly.)

Choosing her name allowed for a double in-joke. "McCoy" is an homage to the historic family of the same name, although Nurse McCoy is from a different part of Appalachia and would deny kinship with them or any part in their infamous feud with the Hatfields. Shortly after choosing the name for this reason, I realized it could also be considered a fun reference to another fictional healer: Dr. McCoy, from Gene Roddenbury's *Star Trek*.

As to what Hettie herself would think of this long, drawn-out explanation of her origins, she'd probably tell me to stop jawing and get supper on the table. After all, she's a nurse, not a historian.

Victorian nurses wearing nursing chatelaines

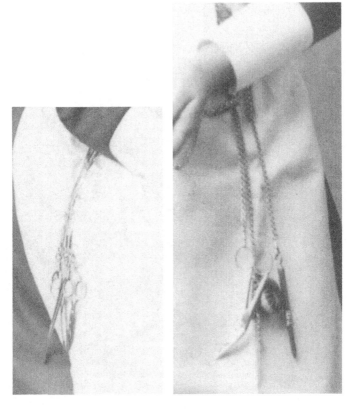

Details of nursing chatelaines from the picture on the previous page.

Appendix III
Sources related to Victorian medicine

—The descriptions of McCoy's duties when she was a ward nurse in a hospital were based on information regarding the duties of nurses found in "Occupations of for Women", *The Woman's Book, Volume I*, New York: Charles Scribner's Sons, 1894. pp. 41-44.

—Dashing cold water upon the face of someone having hysterics when no other treatment proves successful was suggested by Mrs. Beeton's *The Book of Household Management*, Ward, Lock & Bowden, Ltd. London: 1893, p. 1595.

—*Viburnum prunifolium* and a mustard plaster between the shoulders as treatments to prevent miscarriage appear in Montgomery, E.E., M.D. "Sepsis Following Abortion, and Its Treatment: Clinical Lecture Delivered at the Philadelphia Hospital." *International Clinics: A Quarterly of Clinical Lectures*. Ed. Judson Daland, M.D. et al. J.B. Lippincott Company, Philadelphia, 1894. A digitized copy of the article can be read at http://tinyurl.com/hnzjnpe

—The description of McCoy making a mustard plaster was based on instructions in Mrs. Beeton's *The Book of Household Management*, Ward, Lock & Bowden, Ltd. London: 1893, p. 1555.

—The "nursing trick" McCoy uses to put Felix under his bed's covers without waking him would have been a variation on the techniques used by trained nurses to change the bedclothes of helpless invalids without removing them from the bed. These techniques are described in "Hygiene of the Sick-Room. How to Change Bedclothes." *The Woman's Book, Volume I*, New York: Charles Scribner's Sons, 1894. pp. 296-297.

—A reference to messages left for doctors "on the slate which should be kept in every doctor's hall" was found in the article, "In the Sick Room: Helping The Doctor In Fourteen Ways", *Good Housekeeping,* June 7, 1890, p. 55.

Appendix IV
Fraudulent Spiritualists and Esmerelda's Tricks

—The plot of *A Rapping At the Door* was inspired by the non-fiction book, *Spiritualists and Detectives*, by Allan Pinkerton, Trow's Printing and Bookbinding Co.: New York. 1876.

Allan Pinkerton was the founder of the Pinkerton Detective Agency and arguably the most renowned real-life detective of nineteenth-century America. Sherlock Holmes may be slightly better-known now, but Pinkerton and his detective agency were *real*.

A digitized version of a 1905 edition of *Spiritualists and Detective* is available here: http://tinyurl.com/hps8gtg

—The titles listed on Esmerelda's handbill ("Positive, Prophetic...") were taken from a spiritualist's business card described on p. 103 of Pinkerton's book.

—The description of spiritualism as "constant communication between the mortals and the occupants of the beautiful spirit-home beyond the river" is cribbed from Pinkerton's book, p. 59.

—The surname Nettleton was taken from Pinkerton's book; Pinkerton uses it as an alias when writing about a real spiritualist his agency was hired to investigate.

—The 1858 book, *The Sociable: Or, One Thousand and One Home Amusements* describes using a magnet to stop a watch in its final chapter, "Science in Sport, or Parlor Magic" (p. 351.) The trick is effected by the action of the magnet on the watch's balance wheel. The book makes a point of recommending a *small* magnet to avoid permanent damage to the watch; the one used by Esmerelda to stop Mrs. Brown's watch was considerably more powerful.

—The detail about Ken and Addie being reminded of India shawls when they smell patchouly comes from an interesting practice described in F.S. Clifford's *A Romance of Perfumed Lands*. Boston: Clifford & Co., October, 1881, p. 162: "Years ago real India shawls brought an extravagent price and purchasers could always distinguish them by their odor, they being always perfumed with patchouly. The French manufacturers had for some time successfully imitated the India fabric, but could not impart the odor. At length they discovered the secret, and began to import the plant to perfume articles of their own manufacture, and thus palm off home-spun shawls as real India."

(In Clifford's book patchouly was consistently spelled with a "y" instead of the modern spelling "patchouli". I retained Clifford's historical spelling in *A Rapping at the Door*.)

—The incident with the scarf in the dark is based on an account of a false spirit materialization in "Some Famous Exposures." By David P. Abbott, *Library of the World's Best Mystery and Detective Stories*, ed.

Julian Hawthorne, New York: The Review of Reviews, 1907. pp. 277—278. A digital copy of this book is available here: http://tinyurl.com/zslnxnq

—The detail about luminous powder being used in life buoys, moorage buoys, diving and other marine applications was found in *The American Architect and Building News*, May 15, 1880. p. 215—216. A digitized version of the article can be read here: http://tinyurl.com/zrvp7xv

—The detail about heavy perfume being used to disguise the odor of turpentine (used by con artists in the creation of luminous powder for stunts in seances) was found in "How Spirits Materialize." *Library of the World's Best Mystery and Detective Stories*, ed. Julian Hawthorne, New York: The Review of Reviews, 1907. pp. 298—299.

—A description of chemical potassium being used by fraudulent mediums was found in "Fraudulent Spiritualism Unveiled" by David P. Abbot. *Library of the World's Best Mystery and Detective Stories*, ed. Julian Hawthorne, New York: The Review of Reviews, 1907. pp. 241, 247, 248.

—For information on palm reading in the Victorian era, see *The Mysteries of Astrology and the Wonders of Magic* by Dr. C.W. Roback. London: Sampson Low, Son & Company, 1854. pp. 57-63. A digitized copy of this book is available at http://tinyurl.com/jg3fssu

Appendix V
Bon Mots

—The phrase, "giving her head that peculiarly ludicrous inclination that all women affect when they are particularly anxious to be noticed, but also particularly anxious to not have it noticed that they wish to be noticed" was cribbed from Pinkerton's book, p. 216.

—Felix's comment about Esmerelda, "Then she went as far as a naturally shrewd and naturally lewd woman dare go" was cribbed from Pinkerton's book, p. 202.

—McCoy's reflection about Jacob and Addie being good for Silas and giving him "something to do besides imagining that he had every ill under the sun" was partially cribbed from an 1888 article, "Cycling for Women", the full text of which can be read at http://www.thisvictorianlife.com/cycling-for-women.html

—In Chapter XIX of *A Rapping At the Door*, Ken tells Dr. Brown, ""I'm a clerk, not a wharf rat!…It's not like I have to shift boxes of freight around."
    "Wharf rat" was a late 19th-century slang term for a dock laborer in Pacific Northwest ports, according to an exhibit at the Port Gamble Historic Museum.

—The phrases "Dumb it!" and "Goll dumb it!" appear throughout the 1887 comic novel *Shams: Or Uncle Ben's Experiences With Hypocrites*, by John S. Draper, Thompson & Thomas, 1887, 1889 ed. This story relates the various adventures and misadventures of a yokel bumpkin and was a valuable source for late nineteenth-century American slang and colloquial phrases.

—The description of a reporter as "Someone whose business is to stick his nose in everybody else's business, and then run and tell the paper about it before the business is even concluded" is cribbed from *Shams* [ibid.], p. 210.

—The description of a bustle dress having "a wire basket or chicken-coop arrangement in the back of the skirt, to make it have the appearance of a city lot, narrow in front but running back a good ways" was cribbed from *Shams*, [ibid.] p. 258.

—McCoy's monologue about not liking reporters ("I don't hold with newspaper reporters. Y'all are meddlesome, and as a general rule, inclined to tellin' whoppers my six-year-old niece would know better than to believe. And furthermore, I am by general inclination opposed to givin' away the family secrets of the folks I care for, or to lettin' other folks ferret 'em out!") was cribbed and slightly re-worked from *Shams*, [ibid.] p. 350.

—The reference to "a sort of cinnamon-rose blush…
a little nearer on her left ear than her nigh one." was
taken from *Shams*, [ibid.] p. 62.

—The phrase "sweet as a hogshead of Sandwich
Island sugar" was taken from *Shams*, [ibid.] p. 348.
(A hogshead is a large cask holding about sixty three
or sixty four gallons. The Hawaiian archipelago was
formerly known as the Sandwich Islands.)

—Felix's remark, "He's not Rossetti, Ken!…And
remember even he had second thoughts about the
matter." is a reference to an incident in the life of
Dante Gabriel Rossetti. In 1862 when Rossetti's wife
Elizabeth Siddal died of a laudanum overdose
(probably a suicide), Rossetti buried a manuscript of
his poetry in her coffin. Seven years later in a move
offensive to all human decency, Rossetti had Siddal's
body exhumed just to get his manuscript back. In
1928 poet Dorothy Parker summed up the macabre
scene in her own pithy style: "Dante Gabriel Rossetti
/ Buried all of his libretti, / Thought the matter over,
— then / Went and dug them up again."

—The quote on the front endpaper of Jacob's diary
("It is a great advance in civilization to be able to
describe the common facts of life, and…at least an
equal advance to wish to describe them.") is by
Walter Bagehot from *Physics and Politics*, 1872, p.
212. Diarists often record favorite quotes in their
journals; some modern publishers of blank books
intended for journaling even pre-print quotes atop
some of the otherwise blank pages. The front

endpaper of James Eagleson's 1884 diary (archived in Special Collections at the University of Washington) reads, "Webster says, 'History is a continuous narrative of events,' but I include in mine many private thoughts."

—The surname Skinem (given to Charlie Skinem, the ancillary character who Eunice ran off with after she dumped Jacob) was suggested by *Shams* [ibid.] On pages 329—331 of Draper's book, a group of con artists are named Dodgem, Skinem, Ketchem, and Holdem.

—The alias Gracilis is a sideways reference to Esmerelda / Eunice's real surname of Nettleton: *Urtica gracilis* is a subspecies of stinging nettle.

—Spark and Tanglefoot (Felix's writing handle and his nickname for Ken) were both writing handles used by writers for the *Wheel and Cycling Trade Review*, 1889—1890.

Appendix VI
Marriage, Breach of Promise Suits

—Certain portions of McCoy's conversation with Silas about marriage in the story's opening scene were influenced by a conversation in an 1888 piece, "Kitchen Love and Loyalty." The full text of this piece can be read at:
http://www.thisvictorianlife.com/kitchen-love-and-loyalty-fictionmdash1888.html

—Kitty's personal conflict about being a re-married widow was inspired by the plot of Amélie Rives' 1888 book, *The Quick Or the Dead?*

—The story about McCoy's shy cousin Danny being sued for breach of promise to marry by a woman he'd met briefly on a train was inspired by Chapter VII ("I Make A Narrow Escape") in *Blunders of a Bashful Man*, J.S. Ogilvie Publishing Company, New York, 1881.

Breach of promise suits were virtually impossible for a man to disprove, even when the evidence against him was extremely scanty. Between 1816—1850, more than 95% of women claiming breach of promise suits won their cases, and between 1870—1914 the success rates for women in breach of promise suits varied from around 80% to around 90%. (Source: Bates, Denise. *Breach of Promise to*

Marry: A History of How Jilted Brides Settled Scores,
Pen & Sword Books Ltd., England, 2014. p. 103.)

Appendix VII
Notes on Victorian Cycling

—In the high wheel era, the term "header" (active form "take a header") referred to any fall from a bicycle: it did **not** mean falling on one's head, it was simply slang for a crash. It applied equally when the unfortunate Wheelman landed on his hands, his knees, or any other body part. (Similarly, we now use the term "crash" to describe any fall from a bike, even when the actual sound involved is more of a thwack, a thud, or a shriek.) Confusion about terminology led to the widely held misconception that riders who fall off high wheel bicycles frequently fall on their heads, but such a landing is actually extremely rare. In 1883 a medical doctor writing on high wheel bicycles described the actual physiology of a typical fall: "When the wheel meets with any obstruction upon the road, either unobserved by the rider or thrown by some mischievous urchin, the rider is pitched forward upon his hands and knees, in the same way as if he had stumbled while running upon his feet. This is called "taking a header." The wrist is sometimes sprained in these involuntary dismounts, but the rider is never seriously injured unless he is going at an inordinate rate of speed." – Kinch, Charles A., M.D. "A Medical Symposium: The Bicycle and Tricycle for Physicians and Patients." *The Wheelman.* August 1883, p. 362. The full text of this article can be found at http://tinyurl.com/hc9n8yt

—This story has a couple different very oblique homages to Victorian cycling legend Karl Kron, author of *Ten Thousand Miles On A Bicycle.* One of these homages is Felix's reference to "the best bulldog ever". Kron was inordinately fond of his bulldog Curl, and actually dedicated his famous book to his dog.

The second homage is Ken's dislocated elbow: it is the same injury which Kron sustained the very first time he attempted riding an ordinary bicycle.

High-wheel tricycle

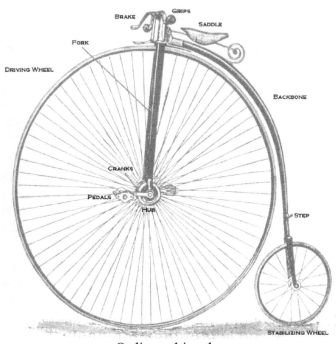

Labels on diagram:
GRIPS
BRAKE
SADDLE
FORK
DRIVING WHEEL
BACKBONE
CRANKS
PEDALS
HUB
STEP
STABILIZING WHEEL

Ordinary bicycle

"…They reached the house and Ken and Felix braced their bikes against each other in the yard…"

Appendix VIII
Miscellaneous Notes

—For more about everyday life in the Victorian era, be sure to check out my website: www.ThisVictorianLife.com.
Inside details of the Tales of Chetzemoka series can be found at http://www.thisvictorianlife.com/tales-of-chetzemoka.html

—A note on names: As general rule, in the nineteenth-century first names were used between friends and family members, and when addressing laborers, low-ranking servants and children. A young housemaid like Mary, who is working at her very first service job and only comes by once a week, is a good example of the sort of low-ranking servant who would be addressed by her first name. Last names were used between acquaintances and when addressing high-ranking servants. Trained nurses, butlers and head housekeepers who supervised other staff in large estates would all be addressed by their last names. There were exceptions to this rule, especially in the casual environment of the American West*, but it's useful as a general guideline when considering the culture.

When Nurse Hettie McCoy reminds Silas to call her McCoy and not Hettie, she's asserting her role in his life. She's uncomfortable with the idea of being elevated to the status of friend or family member, but she won't be demoted to under-servant, either.

Since Book III of the Tales of Chetzemoka is written from Nurse McCoy's perspective, I originally wrote out all the names as she would have addressed people in speech —Mr. Simmons for Jacob, Mr. Kellam for Ken, etc. After careful consideration (and discussion with my husband Gabriel), though, I finally decided that the story would be more readable if the omniscient narrator used mostly first names. The characters are truly becoming dear friends to me as I write these stories, and I want the readers to feel they are likewise on a first-name basis with them.

*Fans of the Chetzemoka series might remember the teamster Ezra Dunn referring to Ken and Felix by their first names in Book II, *Love Will Find A Wheel.* Ordinarily a laborer like Dunn would have called them Mr. Kellam and Mr. Halloway, but even casual acquaintances tend to think of Ken and Felix by their first names because they *act* so young much of the time.

—Hair jewelry of various sorts was very popular in the Victorian era and is still made by specialty artists today. One of my oldest friends is a hair jewelry artist; to see her work go to https://www.etsy.com/shop/WispAdornments

It's been a pleasure sharing this story with you. Watch for the next book in a few months, and best of luck on all your projects! —S.C.

The Tales of Chetzemoka Historical Fiction Series

By Sarah A. Chrisman

In a seaport town in the late 19th-century Pacific Northwest, a group of friends find themselves drawn together —by chance, by love, and by the marvelous changes their world is undergoing. In the process, they learn that the family we choose can be just as important as the ones we're born into. Join their adventures in

The Tales of Chetzemoka

http://www.thisvictorianlife.com/historical-fiction.html

First Wheel in Town
Book I in the Tales of Chetzemoka
http://www.thisvictorianlife.com/first-wheel-in-town.html

In the summer of 1881, a Pacific Northwest town is buzzing with curiosity over a mysterious package received by handsome young Dr. Brown. Kitty Butler, the town dressmaker, is as curious as anyone else. She only knows one thing about that crate in the post office: everyone else's guesses about its contents are all wrong.

When Dr. Brown unpacks the crate and reveals the first bicycle the town has ever seen, he wants to share his enthusiasm for this revolutionary new piece of technology —but encounters overwhelming hostility instead of the excitement he'd expected. The only one who seems positively interested is the pretty young widow Kitty Butler, and Dr. Brown soon realizes how much he needs her support...

Love Will Find A Wheel
Book II in the Tales of Chetzemoka
http://www.thisvictorianlife.com/love-will-find-a-wheel.html

"I'm sure he'll be glad you're here — once he gets used to it."

When Jacob Simmons arrives in Washington Territory in the summer of 1882 and receives a glacial reception from his uncle Silas, he appreciates Dr. Brown's encouraging prediction but doesn't have much faith in it. Jacob's not even sure Silas will have time to get used to his presence, let alone consider him welcome. If the young man can't meet the draconian requirements of a contract with his business investors, he'll face exile and financial ruin, thus fulfilling old Silas' prediction that he would be just as dismal a failure as his father. His whole future rests on finding a market for a remarkable new machine —and he'll need help selling them.

***

Addie Kellam is an incredibly lonely young woman. She's more comfortable with books than with other people, yet she longs for the sort of romance she reads about in stories. It's something she fears she'll never experience herself, since even friendship seems elusive. She envies the camaraderie her brother finds in his cycling club, but the only bicycles in the town of Chetzemoka are specifically designed for men. There aren't any wheels for women anywhere —are there?

A Rapping At The Door
Book III in the Tales of Chetzemoka
http://www.thisvictorianlife.com/a-
rapping-at-the-door.html

When the delivery of a mysterious
letter to Silas Hayes' mansion is
followed by the arrival of a beautiful
young woman who claims she can
communicate with the dead, Nurse
McCoy sniffs trouble in the wind. It's
obvious to her that the newcomer is
after Silas' fortune, but he is helplessly
in awe of the medium's eerily intimate
knowledge of his past and her
seemingly supernatural abilities.
Meanwhile, Kitty Brown's yearning to
reach out to the departed spirit of her
first love is making her push away her
new husband, just when she needs him
the most. The whole situation is a
dreadful mess, and McCoy's got to
straighten it all out before Silas'
nephew and his bride come back from
their honeymoon. Honestly, she
doesn't know how any of the fools in
this world would get along without
her...

Delivery Delayed
Book IV in the Tales of Chetzemoka
http://www.thisvictorianlife.com/delivery
-delayed.html

It's obvious to everyone in the Chetzemoka cycling club that Lizzie and Isaac could make each other very happy —but does anyone really listen to their friends about affairs of the heart? A prim schoolmarm and a stoic steamship captain are hardly the people to discuss their sentiments, especially with each other. The smallest challenges seem like huge obstacles, even with everyone else trying their best to bring them together. When progress finally seems possible, a well-intentioned little girl steps in with the kind of help they'd be better off without. Will the situation be resolved in time, or will Isaac ship out for good?

A Trip and a Tumble

Book V in the Tales of Chetzemoka
http://www.thisvictorianlife.com/a-
trip-and-a-tumble.html

Time for a vacation —step right up! When Felix's newspaper sends him up to Victoria, B.C. to report on a visiting circus Ken inevitably tags along, "like a dutiful puppy", as Addie says. Meanwhile, Jacob's sent north to Victoria as well, as an ambassador for the cycling company he represents. Addie tells him to keep an eye on the chums, but no one ever could keep Ken and Felix from stumbling into scrapes. When a vivacious high-society belle and a surprisingly timid circus bicyclist enter the picture, things heat up quickly. Be prepared for a grand circus pageant —let the show begin!

Made in the USA
Monee, IL
21 March 2021